THRONE OF FURY

KINGDOM OF FAIRYTALES BOOK 3

J. A. ARMITAGE

Edited By Rose Lipscomb

Cover by Enchanted Quill Press

Proof Reader: Tina Merritt

❀ Created with Vellum

KINGDOM OF FAIRYTALES

You all know the fairytales, the stories that always have the happy ending. But what happens after all those storybook characters get what they wanted? Is it really a happily ever after?

In this prequel, you will find out what happens next, be transported back to those lands you fell in love with and be prepared to meet some new characters along the way.

Kingdom of Fairytales is a new way of reading with one chapter a day and one book a week throughout the year beginning January 1st

Lighting-fast reads you won't be able to put down

Read in real time as each chapter follows a day in the life of a character throughout the entire year, with each bite-sized episode representing a week in the life of our hero.

Each character's story wrapped up at the end of every season with a brand new character and story featured in each season.

Fantasy has never been so epic!

READING ORDER

Kingdom of Fairytales is a 52 book series split into thirteen seasons. Each season has a four book story arc of a fairytale character with the last season seeing them all coming together. You can read any series first with the exception of thirteen, however it is recommended that you read in the order below…

PREQUEL

SLEEPING BEAUTY

1. Queen of Dragons
2. Heiress of Embers
3. Throne of Fury
4. Goddess of Flames

LITTLE MERMAID

5. Queen of Mermaids
6. Heiress of the Sea
7. Throne of Change
8. Goddess of Water

RED RIDING HOOD

9. King of Wolves
10. Heir of the Curse
11. Throne of Night
12. God of Shifters

RAPUNZEL

13. King of Devotion
14. Heir of Thorns
15. Throne of Enchantment
16. God of Loyalty

RUMPELSTILTSKIN

17. Queen of Unicorns
18. Heiress of Gold
19. Throne of Sacrifice
20. Goddess of Loss

BEAUTY AND THE BEAST

21. King of Beasts
22. Heir of Beauty
23. Throne of Betrayal
24. God of Illusion

ALADDIN

25. Queen of the Sun
26. Heiress of Shadows
27. Throne of the Phoenix
28. Goddess of Fire

CINDERELLA

29. Queen of Song
30. Heiress of Melody
31. Throne of Symphony

32. Goddess of Harmony

ALICE IN WONDERLAND

33. Queen of Clockwork
34. Heiress of Delusion
35. Throne of Cards
36. Goddess of Hearts

WIZARD OF OZ

37. King of Traitors
38. Heir of Fugitives
39. Throne of Emeralds
40. God of Storms

SNOW WHITE

41. Queen of Reflections
42. Heiress of Mirrors
43. Throne of Wands
44. Goddess of Magic

PETER PAN

45. Queen of Skies
46. Heiress of Stars
47. Throne of Feathers
48. Goddess of Air

URBIS

49. Kingdom of Royalty
50. Kingdom of Power
51. Kingdom of Fairytales
52. Kingdom of Ever After

KINGDOM
OF
FAIRYTALES
URBIS PRISON
SHIPLEY
THE VALE
AZREN
BADALAH
DESERT
KISBU
DRACONIS
ZHORE
MOSA
ABORIA
ELDER
URBIS
AZURE
ENCHANTIA
AIRI
SKYLA
EMERALD CITY
OZ
FLORIS
TULIS
THE FORGE
ARCADIA
RENAIS
MELFALL
ATLANTICE
ANTIA

15TH JANUARY

"Your father wishes to see you. Get out of bed." Dahlia's urgent tone drifted through my dreams of children with golden rings around their irises, children that called to me but were just out of reach. Children that I knew, or at least I felt, I knew.

They evaporated like smoke on the wind as the first tendrils of light invaded my consciousness as Dahlia cruelly opened the curtains, letting the morning in.

I pulled the cover over my head, hoping that if I ignored her, Dahlia would leave me alone. My whole life felt like a lie, and my father was the last person I wanted to speak to. He was one of the people who perpetuated that lie. My mother was the other, but as I could hardly be mad with her right now, I was saving all my anger for my father. My father, whom I'd loved with my whole heart and respected. My father, who was the most wonderful man I knew until the beginning of the year and the return of my mother's curse. Actually, no, his spiral into awfulness had started before that with the plan of marrying me off to a stranger who was at least twice my age and was, at best, a complete jerk.

Dahlia never did have much time for self-pity and whining. She didn't ask me again. She just pulled my covers off, leaving me on the bed, cold in only my nightgown.

The sound of my bath running reminded me that she wouldn't let up until it got to the point where she would literally drag me out of bed and plonk me straight in the bath.

I tried to grab back the memories of my dream, but it was too late. The children were long gone and, along with them, the warmth of wellbeing that I'd gripped to throughout the night.

I shivered as I pulled myself from the comfort of my own bed.

I'd barely slept a wink of sleep, and the few moments I had snatched were punctuated with dreams. Dreams of the brother or sister that I'd just found out about. Someone who looked like me. A twin.

I loved all my brothers, but I'd never really fit in. I was the ugly duckling in a group of beautiful swans. Ok, that was taking it too far, but I didn't look like them. I pulled my nightshirt over my head and settled into the bath, my mind still whirring with the thought that I had a real sibling out there. I had so many questions and no one to ask. Olivie had told me as much as she knew, but it didn't amount to much. She didn't know if my twin was still in Draconis or was somewhere else in another kingdom.

I remembered something Vasuki had told me a week or so earlier. He'd said that I wasn't a whole. That I was a part of something bigger. I don't think he truly understood what that meant any more than I did, but now it made sense. I wasn't a whole. I was one half of a set of twins.

I'd always wanted a sister. Growing up with three brothers had been fun, but I'd have liked another girl to play with. Of course, my twin could easily have been a boy. I wondered if he had golden rings around his irises like I did. If I wasn't the only one.

Rushing downstairs, taking each step two at a time and ignoring the maids who gave me dirty stares as I whipped past them, I raced to my father's office. I found him exactly where I expected to, eyebrows deep in messy paperwork with red rings around his eyes that told me he'd had yet another sleepless night. I wasn't in any mood to feel sorry for him. He'd kept a secret so huge that I was nowhere near close to forgiveness.

He looked up when I entered, paperwork still in his hand. "Azia, you're here. I wanted to speak with you abou..."

"I need to talk to you first," I said, butting in angrily and slamming my hand down on his desk. A few of the papers fluttered, but the huge stack held firm. I would never have done such a thing in the past, but things had changed. I was way past caring what anyone thought of me, and that included my father, the king.

"What is it, Azia?" His voice was weary, the voice of a man with the weight of the world on his shoulders. There was no anger in it, but I could see he didn't need yet another problem to deal with. If it wasn't such a huge deal, I would have left him to his work, but it was a huge deal.

"Why didn't tell me that I had a brother or sister?" I asked, holding him in a cold hard stare.

He raised an eyebrow in askance."I rather thought you would have noticed on your own."

"I'm not talking about Remy or Hollis or Ash. I'm talking about the night I was brought to the castle when I was a baby. Why did you only take me in? Why separate me from my twin?"

He sat straight up in his chair and eyed me with surprise. "What are you talking about?"

"I know," I replied. "There's no point hiding it from me any longer. I know I have a twin."

He shook his head slowly. "I'll overlook the fact that someone has been filling your head with nonsense, and I'll pretend that you are not being incredibly rude right now. Sit down, and I'll tell you what happened the night you came to us." He indicated a chair for me to sit in.

"We've never hidden anything from you, Azia. We decided right from the start that you were our daughter and that you were as important to us as if you were ours by blood. We even made the decision to pass the throne to you rather than one of our natural-born children. If that doesn't show you how much we love you, I don't know what will. We also decided to tell you right from the start that you were adopted. You've always known. I can tell you about the night you came to us if that will make you feel better."

"So tell me," I snapped, taking a seat opposite his.

He waited until I was completely seated and comfortable before he spoke. A frisson of excitement ran through me. I was finally about to find out where I was from. Maybe even who I was.

"Your mother and I were newlyweds," my father began. "Your mother made it no secret that she wanted children. I would have liked to have waited and spend a little time alone with her first, but she was adamant. We adopted you very early on in our marriage. Probably too soon, though I have never regretted it. Not for an instant. You were loved as if you were our own, right from the start."

Nice. Sentimental even, but this isn't what I needed to hear. I needed facts. "I was told that when I was brought to the house, there was another baby. It was heard crying."

He held my gaze. "I don't know of any other baby, Azia. There was never any other child. There was only ever you. Not long after you came, your mother fell pregnant with

Remy. He, along with Hollis and Ash, are our biological children. Your mother always told me she was so glad we adopted you, or she'd be in a house filled with boys."

Frustration gripped me. "So why was another baby heard crying?"

My father rubbed his temples and sighed. "I don't know, Azia. Perhaps the adoption agency people were on their way to deliver another baby to another set of parents. It doesn't mean that the other baby was your twin. Plenty of infants are born in Zhore. Does that answer all your questions?"

I nodded slowly. He was right. Of course, an adoption agency might very well have been carrying more than one child to more than one set of parents. Why hadn't I thought of that? I'd not thought of it, because it didn't feel right. It didn't explain the gnawing in my gut when I thought about another child. It didn't explain my dreams. It didn't explain the fact that I felt less than whole.

"Well then," he said, going back to his paperwork. "I'll need you to finalize the plans for this ridiculous competition you've decided to stage. The Sentinel has been on my case, and all my administrative staff are busy fielding calls about what's going to happen rather than doing the job I pay them for. It really is a nuisance."

"I'm sorry, Father," I said, standing up.

I swirled the new information around in my mind as I walked back to my room. It was entirely plausible that Olivie had heard another baby that had nothing to do with me. Maybe it was a pipe dream, a delusion of an adopted child that there would be others out there who looked like me.

Still, it didn't sit well in my stomach. My father had all the answers, but I didn't believe him. There was nothing he said that didn't make sense, but there was a tell in his eye as he spoke. The way he blinked a little too rapidly. The way he rubbed his fingers together as he told me that I was the only baby. Taking a detour, I headed not upwards to my bedroom, nor to the library to come up with plans for the competition, but down to the rooms beneath the castle. We had a wine cellar down there that I was sorely tempted to visit, but there was also something down there that I needed to see more. The royal vaults.

A huge metal door hid rooms upon rooms of treasure and gifts given to the royal family for generations. My brothers and I often played hide and seek down there before Hollis accidentally knocked over and smashed a vase worth a fortune. After that, the royal children were banned, but I was no longer a child. and what was more, I didn't need a password to get in. The vault was guarded by two armed guards, plus the keeper of the vault, who was more of custodian than guard.

Having had no reason to come down to the vault since the vase incident, five or six years before, I'd only seen the keeper of the vault in passing since then.

Taking the steps two at a time, I came to a stop by the antique wooden desk in front of the huge metal door flanked by two guards in uniform.

"Good morning," I said, nodding to them before turning my attention to the keeper. He eyed me suspiciously, looking up from a huge book filled with entries of all the people who had been in and out of the vault and the times, dates, and reasons for each visit. Next to it, sat a pot of ink and a well-used quill.

He was meticulous and proud of his job. He also hated me and my brothers for bringing shame on him when we'd broken the vase. He took looking after the contents of the vault very seriously.

"Your Highness," he said, giving me a wary smile and a small bob of the head. "How may I help you this fine day?"

Wisps of thinning white hair covered his head, with bald

patches shining through. He'd been here a long time, and it showed. His ink marked hands were covered with paper-thin skin, which showed his age. Not that he needed to be particularly fit or strong. That was the guard's job, which was just as well considering he looked like he'd throw his back out just picking up a pen.

"I'd like to go in the vault, please, Hestor."

Pursing his lips, he appeared to be pondering my request. I held my breath, waiting for the inevitable rejection, but it seemed he'd softened in his old age. He picked up a quill and dipped it in his ink well before writing my name in his book next to the time and date.

I would have preferred to have no account of this, but people came into and out of the vault all the time, so it wouldn't be long before my name was hidden down the list.

"And my I ask your reason for visiting the vault today?" he asked, raising a watery eye toward me. "I'm assuming that hide and seek is no longer on the agenda."

My mouth twisted up at the corners. He was teasing me. Maybe he wasn't the miserable old git I'd pegged him for all those years ago.

Not wanting to tell him the real reason, I made something up on the spot. Something I hoped sounded believable.

"There is to be a photoshoot of me for the Royal Competition for the Draconian Sentinel. I'd like to make it an official photograph, and I believe I should look regal. I'd like to take one of my mother's necklaces."

Licking his lips, he held the quill to the paper but paused. "And is there nothing suitable in your mother's room for you to borrow?"

Shaking my head, I readied the lie on my lips. My mother kept a lot of jewelry in her room. She hated coming down to the vault, but some of the jewels we owned were too precious to have lying around. The more formal jewelry, along with the expensive pieces and the royal crown jewels were kept down here behind lock and key.

"There is a piece I had in mind, and I can't find it in her room. I don't really want to be messing around in her things as she sleeps."

I put on the saddest face I could muster, hoping to appeal to his sympathy. My mother was cursed after all.

"I quite understand," he replied, licking the end of the quill then writing the word necklace down in the book. "As you require something of such value, I will be required to come into the vault with you and send you on your way with one of the guards until the necklace is brought back safely."

Panic shot through me. The last thing I needed was having Hestor follow me through the vault.

"That isn't necessary. I know where the necklace is. I can find it myself."

"Nevertheless," he said, pulling his bony body into a standing position. "My job is to keep the vault and make sure nothing goes missing. Having a thing of such value will put your own life at risk too, Your Highness. Besides, I need to write the tag number down in my book so nothing goes missing."

Damn. I'd forgotten that everything down there was tagged and cataloged with a number.

He pulled a key from a chain around his neck and inserted it into a lock holding the huge vault door shut before turning a small dial with numbers on it. He shielded it from my sight as he turned it left and right. A click indicated the vault was unlocked.

The two guards pulled it open for us with a high-pitched creak, and a wave of musty air hit me in the face, making me cough.

Hestor shuffled in, leaving me to follow in his wake.

The vault was separated into sections. Large items of

value, such as furniture and statues, were cataloged and stored in a large room to the right. The higher up maids with clearance would often come down here to remove items to change the look of the palace at my mother's whims. I followed Hestor to a massive metal cage where he, once again, pulled the key out and unlocked the door that would take us to the most restricted part of the vault. The place where the jewelry was kept, the home of the crown jewels and paperwork of national importance. Not many had clearance for this part of the vault, and I was surprised that Hestor even contemplated letting me in. But then again, he knew as well as I did, the emotional state of my father right now, and though I'd played around down here in the past, I was an adult now and a member of the royal family. He probably thought it wise to just let me do what I wanted. Not that he trusted me completely. He walked right next to me the whole time, not taking his eyes off me for a second. Not wanting to arouse his suspicion, I went straight to the glass cases with necklaces in them. I didn't care which one I took. It didn't matter. I pretended to deliberate over them while trying to come up with a plan to get to the paperwork.

I knew where the family documents were kept. On the other side of the cage was a huge office with two leather chairs, a desk, and rows upon rows of cabinets. Most were filled with documents relating to the kingdom, but one end was reserved for family matters. The problem was, how was I supposed to get the documents while Hestor was watching my every move?

I fingered one of the necklaces. There was no way Hestor wouldn't notice me crossing the room and rifling through the documents, and if he did see me, he would run straight to my father.

Picking the necklace up, I held it to my neck before putting it back in its case.

I was just about to pick up the next one when a crash made me jump.

Hestor's head swiveled quickly towards the source of the noise.

It was a maid, trying to pick up one of the larger chairs from the other side of the main room.

"You shouldn't be trying to carry that by yourself!" Hestor shouted before muttering under his breath, "Silly girl."

He ran toward her, waving his arms around.

I made use of the diversion, running silently to the desk. Reading down the cabinets, which were all labeled in the same handwriting as Hestor's book outside, I came to the cabinet that said family documents. Four drawers full of the royal family history, but they had dates on them. The top drawer was the most recent. taking a quick peek at Hestor, who was busy arguing with the girl, I pulled the top drawer open. My heart fell when I saw no documents, but a safe instead. A safe with another combination lock on it.

I sucked in a breath, my heart hammering. Hestor wouldn't be with the maid for long, but there was no way he'd tell me the combination.

I stepped back and closed my eyes. My father would have picked the combination to this lock. There was every chance that Hestor didn't even know it. This safe was a personal safe and had nothing to do with the rest of the kingdom. This was for family.

Taking a deep breath, I held my hand out to the lock. There was only one conceivable number I could guess. If I was wrong, I'd never get it right. I turned the dial, this way and that, putting in four numbers. 1004, my mother's birthday. The safe clicked, and the door opened.

At the other end of the room, I could hear Hestor calling in the guards to help him with the chair. This was my only chance, and I had to be quick.

There was very little in the safe, so I pulled the lot out. On the top, was my parent's wedding certificate. Below it, were the birth certificates of both my parents, Remy, Hollis, and Ash. Beneath Ash's birth certificate, I found nothing else. That was it. I rifled through them again, but again I came up with only the six documents. My pulse raced as I checked out the rest of the safe. There were my grandfather's ring and a bundle of letters tied together with a pink ribbon. Stashing the documents back, I pulled out the letters, but a quick rifle through them was enough to see that they were love letters between my parents from the early days in their marriage when my father had to go on royal trips without her. I quickly scanned a couple, but it was plain that they weren't about me. My name was mentioned a couple of times, but only my father asking my mother to kiss me and Remy goodnight for him. I guess they were written when we were young. Apart from a lot of declarations of love, there was nothing in there that would tell me about my past.

Which begged the question. Where was my birth certificate, and why wasn't it with the others?

Even if I was a found child with no birth certificate who'd been handed into the adoption agency, there should still be records of my adoption. But there wasn't. I didn't exist anywhere on paper.

"Sorry about that, Your Highness."

Hestor trooped back into the caged room just as I grabbed the first necklace. "I'll take this one. Thank you." I rushed past him, taking the necklace with me, my emotions in turmoil.

"Just a minute," he called out. "You can't go without a guard!" I halted on the stairs to the main floor of the castle. If I ran off with the necklace now, he'd be on my case forever. Even though I was desperate to be off, I waited for him, tapping my toe on the stone slab floor.

"You know what," I said, handing him back the necklace as he wheezed through the vault door. "I've changed my mind." The last thing I needed was to have a guard following my every move. Especially considering what I planned to do next. "I'll just take one from my mother's room after all."

He gave me a curious look but didn't question me as I bounded up the stairs and away from the vault.

I had no identity. I was no one. I belonged nowhere. I may or may not have had a secret brother or sister. I wanted to march back into my father's study and confront him, but then he would know I'd been snooping. Besides, if he found out, he'd almost certainly stop me from doing what I planned to do next. Actually, scrap that, he would definitely stop me.

I ran up the stairs to my room to pick up a shawl that would cover my head. Where I was going, I didn't want anyone to recognize me. As I came up to the corridor, I ran straight into Dahlia.

"There you are," she said in a testy tone. "I've scoured the castle looking for you. Where have you been? Actually, never mind, as long as you're here now. Come with me. I have a job for you."

"I was going to...go for a nap." I didn't want Dahlia to know where I was going any more than I did my father.

"It's nine o'clock in the morning!" she said, grabbing my hand. "I'm sure you can stay awake long enough to help me with this little task. You can nap after we are done."

The little task turned out to be a fitting for my wedding dress, followed by the planning of the wedding itself.

"Is this really necessary?" I asked as a seamstress measured me. "I don't even have a husband-to-be yet."

Dahlia nodded. "Yes, it's necessary. The wedding is coming up in a couple of weeks. and you might not have a husband-to-be yet, but you will have. You need a dress. Once we've done here, we'll be doing a cake tasting and then picking some wedding flowers. I asked Caspian to come and help."

My face contorted into a look of distaste. "Why?"

"Because he will probably be the one to end up marrying you. As much as I'll be cheering my son on at the competition, he's an oaf, and I doubt he'll make it through the first round. He was only considered for the competition at all because I put his application in the yes pile when the secretaries weren't looking."

"There is a yes pile?" I asked. I'd not put much thought into the admin behind the competition. "That must mean there is a no pile."

"Of course, there is," she said, holding a material sample up to me. "Satin or silk?"

"I thought the competition was open to everyone. How is there a no pile if anyone can enter?"

"Silk, I think," she said, handing the sample to the seamstress who was now writing down the measurements in her book with a pencil.

"We've had over fifteen thousand applications. There just isn't time to have everyone enter. It would take weeks if not months."

"Fifteen thousand?" I asked weakly. "Fifteen...thousand!"

"Yes, that's what I said."

"No sitting down!" the seamstress screeched as I tottered. "We are not finished yet."

"What do you think about pink for the bridesmaids?" Dahlia asked, holding up another sample. My mind reeled with the sheer size of this thing, and my stomach groaned from the lack of breakfast. I'd been so busy, I'd forgotten to have any.

"I don't care," I said. "How are these fifteen thousand men being whittled down?"

"Oh, it's not just men. We've had plenty of women apply too."

I rolled my eyes. The whole thing was a joke. I almost regretted opening up the competition, but if I hadn't, I would have definitely had to marry Caspian. The way things were going, I wasn't sure what was worse. I still hadn't come up with what exactly the competition would entail. A sneaky part of my mind wondered if I could get away with requiring that the competition could only be won by someone whose name was Milo. But knowing my luck, there'd be a thousand Milos entering, and most of the others would change their names. Urgh!

"So how do these people end up on the no pile?" I questioned, ignoring the pink samples Dahlia was waving at me. Whatever way it was, I was going to make sure a few more would be added.

"Well," she began, sorting the pink samples from the purple. "First of all, anyone under eighteen has been immediately disqualified. My son is almost eighteen, so I doubt anyone will notice. Anyone over the age of sixty, too."

"Ah-ha!" I said, jumping on it. "That rules out Caspian. He's a fae and fae are all really old." Probably.

"I checked with him," Dahlia tutted. "He's fifty-one, but he doesn't look a day over twenty-five does he?" She swooned. "I don't know why you didn't just marry him when you got the chance. He's delectable."

"I thought you didn't like him now?" She changed her mind more often than she changed her underwear when it came to Caspian. She'd caught him out in a lie only last week and told me that she thought him untrustworthy. Now she thought he was delectable. I couldn't keep up.

"Not really," she admitted, "but he's a dream to look at, and that's half the battle."

"Hmm," I said unconvinced. "What else?"

"We took the women out too. I don't want to be sexist, but I have a feeling that you'd prefer to marry a man?"

I'd prefer to marry a troll over Caspian, but I nodded my head anyway. "Is that it?"

"No. They had to be physically capable of coming to the castle on the day of the competition too, but that's about everything. It's whittled it down to just over nine hundred, but there are still applications coming in."

"Great," I barked. "Nine hundred men, only two of which actually know me personally, and one of them I detest."

"My gorgeous bride to be!" I swiveled my head to Caspian, who had just walked in the door. "Are you finished in here, because the caterers have just brought in the cakes, and I must say, they look delicious."

Breathing back despair, I knew I wasn't going to be able to put my plan into action today. It would have to wait. I was still going to find out who I was and where I came from. I'd just have to eat a lot of cake first.

16TH JANUARY

After an excruciating day spent with Caspian yesterday, I was all the more determined to get out of the castle today. I went for breakfast as normal, not wanting to arouse suspicion. Once again, it was only Remy and I at the table. At least, he'd perked up a bit. He ate his food quickly as though he didn't have a care in the world. Of course, he didn't. He knew nothing of what was going on. The only thing he understood was the fact that our mother didn't play with him anymore. I could see the sadness in his eyes, and yet, he went about doing things the same as always. His governess had stepped up to the role of mother. I'd seen her spending more time with him than usual. It wasn't the same, but she was doing a brilliant job, and at least, I didn't have to worry about him on top of everything else.

"Aza. Go Zor?"

My heart flipped when I heard his question. He was asking me if I was going to go to Zhore, and that's exactly where I was planning to go. If Remy had figured it out, then so would someone else. But how did Remy know? I'd told no one, not even Milo. I'd not even seen Milo since deciding to go.

"Olly Polly,"

"Oh, you want to go and see Olivie again?" I breathed out a sigh of relief. He wanted to repeat our trip to see his old nanny again. "Not today, buddy, I have things to do."

He cast his eyes downward, tugging at my heartstrings. "I tell you what. When I'm done, we'll spend the evening together? I'll read to you."

He grinned up at me, his face brightening immediately. "Ya, Aza."

I smiled, the first smile I'd managed in days that wasn't plastered on for the sake of other people. "I'll come find you, ok?"

He nodded enthusiastically.

Taking an apple from the fruit bowl at the center of the table, I headed out of the castle, going the back way through the garden door.

I was going to Zhore, but I wasn't going to see Olivie. She'd already told me everything she could. I couldn't trust my father to tell me the truth, so I was going to have to find the truth out for myself. I was going to the adoption agency.

I knew of it vaguely in the way I knew where other buildings were in Zhore. As an adopted child, I should have had more curiosity about the place, but it had never really registered as somewhere I might like to visit. Not until now, at least.

I took the quickest path to Zhore that wouldn't lead me directly to a member of my father's guard. It meant jumping over some walls and running through fields, but the cloak over my head wasn't much of a disguise, and I needed for no one to find out.

I contemplated heading to Milo's house first. I'd never

walked around Zhore or any other place on my own before, but this was something I needed to do myself.

The adoption agency was part of a children's home in one of the quieter backstreets of Zhore, a beautiful, faded-yellow building with flower baskets hanging by the door. They were currently empty other than a dusting of snow, but I remembered them as being filled with blooms of purple when I'd passed by in the summer when I was in a parade. I'd taken note of the sign outside, the Zhore Home for Children and Adoption Agency, but I'd filed it away in the back of my mind, not realizing I'd need to know it so soon.

I stole in, quietly making sure no one on the street was watching me. The street was quiet, and no one paid me any mind as I hurried through the front door. A long corridor led off ahead of me with an open reception area to my right.

"How may I help you?" asked a woman with graying hair and glasses that hung around her neck on a chain. She was the quintessential grandma figure with soft features and kind eyes. Perfect for someone working in a children's home.

My heart beat quicker as I realized I was about to find out who I really was, where I'd come from, maybe even who my real parents were. "I'm here about adoption," I said, keeping my voice low. I felt ashamed to be even asking after how well my parents had treated me. "Specifically, about finding an adopted person's birth parents."

"Of course," she replied with a smile. "Anyone over the age of eighteen is able to come back to us and look at their notes. Of course, sometimes the child's birth parents give false names or don't leave a name at all. I wouldn't want you to be disappoint..."

I pulled my cloak down, exposing who I was. She stopped mid-sentence and dropped into an awkward curtsey, half on and half off the chair.

"Your Royal Highness, it' is an honor."

I stepped up to the counter that separated us and spoke in a quiet voice.

"As you can probably understand, I'd prefer to do this in private."

The sound of a child laughing came along the corridor, making both of us swivel our heads and was quickly followed by an adult's voice shouting, Timmy, after him.

"Yes, of course..." the receptionist said. "Follow me."

She pulled a door in the counter open, and I stepped through to her side. She took me through a door labeled Office, closing it behind us.

The cozy office was everything I'd hope for in an office for a children's home. Photos of kids and babies lined the walls along with thank you cards and letters. Potted plants lined the window sill behind the desk, and a row of cabinets stood against the right hand-wall,

"You asked about adoption. Who did you want to find out about?" she asked, indicating a seat for me to sit in. "Some coffee? Tea perhaps? I could ask my assistant, Jeanette, to bring some."

"That won't be necessary, but thank you. I'm actually here about me."

Confusion knotted her face as she sat in the only other seat in the room. "You?"

I nodded my head and tried to ignore the flutters of excitement in my stomach. I'd been here. I'd spent the first few days of my life within these walls. "Yes, I'd like access to my files, please."

She shook her head. "I don't understand. I have no files on you."

Her words hit me like an out-of-control carriage.

"But, I'm adopted," I said as though that was all she needed to know.

She nodded slowly. "Yes, I know, but you were never here. You never passed through our doors."

I knotted my eyebrows together. "Are you sure? It was about eighteen years ago. I was very tiny. A newborn. I was probably born in late December."

She sucked in a breath and drummed her fingers on the desk as she spoke. "I've worked here for twenty-five years. I remember the news reports about your adoption like it was yesterday. I also remember discussing it with some other staff members, and if you'll forgive me, we all said it was a shame you didn't come from here because your father would have made a nice donation."

Her cheeks turned pink at the admission, and I was positive she was telling me the truth. But I'd trusted people before, and I needed to see for myself.

"Please, may I look in your files?"

She nodded quickly, standing from her chair and hurrying over to the filing cabinets. "Usually, I don't let anyone come in and look at the files. They have to be either one of the parents involved or one of the children, and even then, we have protocol. I hope you understand I'm letting you look because you are a member of the royal family."

"Thank you," I said, feeling guilty. I was going against everything she stood for, but she was too afraid of saying no to a royal. She opened one of the cabinets and pulled out all the files from the year I was born, fanning them out in front of me on the desk.

"Please, can you take the year after ones out too. I was born in this year but was adopted just after. There's a possibility I may have been put in the wrong file."

It was unlikely, but I didn't want to miss something important for the lack of thoroughly checking.

"They are listed in date order," she explained. "The next

filing cabinet along has copies of the same files but in alphabetical order. I assure you the files are exact copies, though."

I sighed, knowing I'd have to go through both. I couldn't chance missing something.

"I have a list of all the names of the children and the parents if you would like to check that first," she said, bringing out a thick leather-bound book. "It only holds the name of the adoptive parents though and not the name of the birth parents. That information is only in the files."

I thanked her and pulled the first pile over to me. There were only five adoptions in the last month of the year I was born, so the daunting task I had thought was actually not so bad. The first file was a baby boy born in the first week of October. The next three were girls, but they looked to be sisters aged three, six, and seven. The last was another baby boy. None of them was me. I moved on to the next pile and checked out the first two weeks of January. This time, there was only one, a nine-year- old boy.

"Is there any way a file could be missing?" I asked in frustration.

She shook her head and held the book she was looking at out to me. "No mistake. You can see here the names and ages of the children that left us around that time. They all corroborate the files."

Frustration overwhelmed me. I had to be from here—just had to be; otherwise, where had I come from? I couldn't have just appeared out of thin air.

"Were you in charge back then?" I asked. "Was there a chance that someone higher up than you kept it secret? I mean, what with my parents being who they are? My adoption could have been written down somewhere else."

She shook her head again. "I'm sorry. I told you, I remember that time like it was yesterday. Your adoption dominated the papers. It was huge news so soon after the royal wedding. There were no babies brought to us in December or January that year. None in November either. We did have a baby girl come in late October, but she stayed with us until she was adopted in the summer. I happen to know her still, so that couldn't be you either. As you saw for yourself, the only babies we adopted out in that time period were boys."

"Is there another adoption agency in town?" I sighed. I needed to get to the bottom of this.

She shook her head, a look of almost pity in her eyes. "No. I'm sorry. We are the only one. There is one about three hundred miles south in Jeeka, but that's the nearest one to us. I know the woman who runs it. I could send a letter to her if you like?"

It made no sense. Why would my parents travel three hundred miles to Jeeka when there was an adoption agency here? She'd just told me that there was a baby girl living here in the winter of the year I was born. Why didn't they take her?"

"No, thank you. Did my parents ever come and visit the agency here?"

"No," she shook her head again. "I would have remembered."

Once again, I was left without answers, and now I had hit a brick wall to find them. I couldn't think of a single reason my parents would travel to Jeeka without first visiting this agency. So the question remained. Who was I, and where had I come from?

"Maybe I will have that coffee after all," I said to the woman feeling utterly dejected. Either no one knew about my birth and adoption, or if they did know, they weren't telling. I had a feeling that this woman was telling the truth. She had no reason to do otherwise, and she seemed genuinely surprised by my questions.

"Of course." She gave me another curtsey as she left me in the room alone. I trusted her, but while she was out, I decided to look through her other files. The book that still lay on the desk told me nothing, and a quick check of her desk drawers brought up no secrets beyond her love of cheesy romance novels. All the cabinets were unlocked, and a quick peek in all of them brought up nothing more than more files. Years of babies' and children's information. Every baby but me.

By the time she came back five minutes later with a mug of coffee and some biscuits, I knew that I'd find out no more here. I did consider a trip to Jeeka, but even as I thought about it, I dismissed the idea out of hand. It made no sense for my parents to travel three hundred miles when there was a perfectly good orphanage here. It made no sense because they hadn't. I'd come to them from somewhere else, but where, and more importantly, how could I find out?

As I sipped on the coffee, I pondered my next move. Someone had to know something about my birth. I had a birth mother and father out there somewhere, but I could hardly ask them. They had not come and asked after me in eighteen years...at least, I didn't think they had. My own parents couldn't help. My mother was asleep, and my father wasn't being entirely honest. Dahlia refused to help me, and so there was nobody left to ask.

Leaving the orphanage had me feeling even more dejected. It had been a colossal waste of time. I walked through the streets of Zhore, my hood over my head so no one would see who I was. I wanted to hide from everyone. It was only when I was almost at the edge of town when inspiration struck. The newspaper! They knew everything, and anything they didn't know, they would do anything to find out. The headquarters of the Draconian Sentinel was in the main part of town, just a few streets over from Milo's house.

I couldn't go and ask the press if they knew about my history, but Milo could.

Running through the streets as the snow once again began to fall, I came to Milo's house and knocked on his door. I'd not seen him at the castle for days, so the likelihood was that he would be working today, but he opened the door. When he saw it was me, he pulled me inside.

"What's the matter?" he asked, the worry in his eyes, matching my own state of excited panic.

"So, the world is falling to pieces, right?" I began in a wheeze, pulling the cloak off.

He took it from me and hung it on a hook. "I guess you could say that," he answered slowly. "Yes."

"And we think it has something to do with my history, " I continued in an excited babble.

Milo shrugged. "Maybe."

I ignored the reticence in his voice and answer and told him what I knew.

"I wasn't adopted from the only adoption agency in town," I began, then proceeded to tell him everything I'd learned in the past few hours, which was precisely zilch.

"I want you to go to the Sentinel and ask to see everything they have on my adoption. I can't go because they'll plaster my face across the front page."

Holding my fingers up to perform air quotes, I spoke again. "Princess seeks truth in adoption scandal."

Milo laughed. "Okay, I see your point, but why would they let me look at their records? They don't know who I am."

"It doesn't matter," I explained. "Their records are open to the public. I know because my parents and I took a tour of the building when it added a new extension last year. They told me all about it. There's a huge room with files, and anything that's not undergoing an active investigation anymore can be viewed by anyone who wants to see it. The best part is, no one will know. There are rows of files, and as long as you don't sneak them out, no one will be the wiser."

"Okay, I'm going," Milo said as I hurried him out of his own house. If my father came here again and found me here alone, he would skin both Milo and me alive, but it was a risk I was willing to take. Besides, there was nowhere I'd rather be than Milo's comfy house away from the madness that was the castle at the moment. Here, I could sit back on his sofa and read his books, admiring the intricacy of the weapons on the walls. Here, there was no one to annoy me, no one to demand that I go here or do that. There was no one here at all, now that Milo had left, and that was the way I liked it. Peace with only my thoughts for company.

At least, that's what I hoped, but less than half an hour after Milo had left, there was a knock at the door. I hadn't even realized how worked up I'd been, but the sound of the slow knock, spiked terror in my heart. After a few deep breaths, I reasoned that if it was my father's guard out looking for me, he would have rapped on the door with much more force.

Frowning, I walked to his door, wondering if I should open it or just wait. Rocking on my feet, I waited, deliberating my next course of action. I had no reason to open the door. Whoever it was, was not here to see me. They would be here for Milo, and Milo wouldn't be back for at least an hour. Deciding to pretend there was no one home, I turned on my heel, but the knocking came again, more insistent this time.

"I know you're here, Azia."

My stomach tensed at the sound of my name. No one called me by my first name beyond my immediate family. To the staff and to the public, I was always addressed as Your Highness. I didn't like it, but that was just the way it was. The only staff member beyond Milo that addressed me as Azia was Dahlia, and that was only because she'd been with me for so long. I knew without certainty that this was not Dahlia behind the door.

Gulping back a breath, I made the decision to leave the door closed. Derillen was still out there somewhere, and although she'd targeted my mother again this time, I knew in my gut that she wanted me.

As I turned to walk away, the door burst open, sending a flurry of snow in its wake.

The shiver passing through me had nothing to do with the cold, however, and everything to do with the wizened old woman standing at the door. It was the woman who'd spoken to me in the Dragon Roost Inn over a week ago. The one who'd told me I was full of power and then promptly disappeared. Gladys something. I'd forgotten about her because not long after, a dragon had flown down the street blowing fire. That was enough to put anything before it from my mind.

"Aren't you going to invite me in, Deary?" she asked, shuffling past me and not waiting for an answer.

I tried to block her, but something stopped my feet from moving, whether magic or fear, I did not know.

She ambled past, not a care in the world, and sat down on the sofa where I'd been sitting mere moments ago.

"Are you coming in or not, Deary, because that pile of snow is only going to get bigger the longer you stand there."

Feeling down to my side, I realized I'd left my sword at the castle, not thinking I'd have a need for it. Milo's walls were filled with swords. One of those would have to do.

Closing the front door, I ran back to the living area and pulled a sword from the wall, leveling it at the witch.

"Get out of here," I said with a shaky voice.

She looked up at me through watery gray eyes. "Why ever would you point a sword at me, Deary? I'm here to help you."

I held the sword firm. "I don't need your help, Derillen."

I swear, I was seconds from ramming the sword through her heart when she began to laugh. A creaky laugh of old age.

"You think I'm that witch? No wonder your heart is racing nineteen to the dozen. Come sit beside me. I'm no witch, and I'm certainly not Derillen. I'm a seer. My name is Gladys."

I hesitated. Derillen was hardly likely to tell me the truth about herself, especially when the sharp end of a sword was inches away from her heart, but then if she was a witch out to kill me, why hadn't she done it already?

I remembered the cloying tendrils of magic trying to invade my brain the day I was in the wool shop. The urgency in which I desperately needed to touch the needle of the spindle. I felt none of that now. Fear, perhaps, but it was all me. This woman was not compelling me to do anything, and the low hum of magic did not reside within her. I lowered the sword and sat in a chair opposite her. She might not be Derillen, but she knew who I was, and I was way past trusting anyone these days. I kept the sword at my side, firmly gripping it in my hand.

"You knew I was here."

The old lady nodded. "I did. Since the moment I met you, your power has intrigued me. I did not know who you were back then. I only thought you were a friend of that boy, Milo. I've seen you a lot in the newspaper since. I never saw you before because you were always standing behind your mother in the pictures. Why was that?"

"Erm...My mother was...is Sleeping Beauty. No one wants to see me when she is around."

The old woman nodded thoughtfully. "You put yourself down. You are a pretty young thing. Certainly, Milo seems to think so."

I blushed at the sound of his name. I knew he liked me.

He showed me all the time, but it was different hearing it from someone else. It made it all the more real somehow.

My nerves around this woman faded somewhat. Not enough to loosen my grip on the sword, but enough to listen to what she had to say. And calling me a pretty young thing aside, I felt that she might be able to tell me something.

"Thank you. May I ask you why you are here?"

"I came to warn you, child," she said, sitting forward on the sofa. "Who you are is connected to everything that is going on around us."

"I know. I figured that out, but I don't know who I am. I'm adopted, but no one seems to know where I came from, or at least no one is telling me. Do you know?"

She shook her head. "I do not know where you came from, but it isn't from around here. You were born a long way from this place. Your aura doesn't resonate like the others. You are a displaced child, taken from your home."

She made it sound so much more spooky than adoption, but she was right. I did feel displaced.

"My mother and father adopted me when I was a newborn," I explained. "They didn't even know exactly how old I was. Just a few weeks at most."

"And you never wondered why?" she asked, raising her eyebrows. "Even adopted children know their own birthdays."

"I want to know," I said urgently. "I want to know everything."

"Of course, you do," she replied, nodding her head slowly. "How about you whip me up a cup of tea, and I'll tell you what I know."

With my heart beating faster, this time with the thrill of excitement rather than fear, I walked into Milo's kitchen and made us both a cup of tea. As the kettle boiled, I kept my eye on the old woman. She sat, hunched over, her gnarled hands on her knees. She was tiny on the sofa, and yet appearances could be deceptive. I already knew that Derillen could change her appearance. I brought the cup out to her, which she accepted gratefully.

As I sipped on my tea, she began to talk. It was almost as if she was telling a story rather than telling me things about my life.

"I cannot tell you anything about your birth," she said, "but I know that you are special. Much more special than a mere princess. You have power that you don't even understand yet, and as the days and weeks pass, it will only grow stronger. I told you before that you are only part of a whole. You will need the other parts to reach your potential."

"I think I have a twin," I said, sitting forward, sloshing my tea everywhere.

Excitement flooded through me at the thought this woman might shed some light on it.

"Hmmm, maybe, maybe not. I cannot say."

Right. Maybe not, then.

"You are a long way away from that which will bind you," she continued. " You will soon be going on a long journey to find out who you are. You will face untold dangers, but you will have a friend by your side."

"Milo?"

She thought for a minute, then shook her head. "I cannot see clearly, but you will trust this person with your life and your secrets. Milo is not the one."

I thought of all the people who I would trust with my life and my secrets. It wasn't a huge list. Milo was the only person I could think of who fit the bill beyond Dahlia, and I couldn't see her coming on a journey with me.

"The kingdom will become very dark," she continued. "We are coming up on a grave time indeed. You, yourself, will not be able to stop the forces gathering power, but I believe for every dark force, there is a person who will be able to combat that force. I wonder if you are a part of that?"

She drank the rest of the tea down and stood up. Without a goodbye, she began to shuffle towards the door, leaving me with no real answers and only more questions.

"Hey, wait," I shouted out. "What do you mean? What will happen to me? I'm a part of what?"

"I cannot foresee everything. Your path is not yet written."

Frustration gripped me. She said she'd tell me things about myself, but I was left feeling more confused than ever before.

"You said I was born far away. Can you guess where, at least?"

She laughed her croaky laugh. "Of course, I can guess, but guesses will not help you. It would have had to have been a place of great power. Somewhere where your birth parents could hide you. Have you not ever thought about why your birth is surrounded in secrecy? Maybe that's the part you want to concentrate on rather than where you are from."

She shuffled out into the street, soon to be lost in the swirls of snow. A clap on my back made me jump a mile.

"Milo," I screeched. "You made me jump."

"What are you doing out here? You'll catch your death of cold."

He ushered me back inside and closed the door behind us. Noting the two empty cups, he raised an eyebrow.

"Who was here?"

"You remember the old lady from the pub? Gladys? She came to talk to me. She said she knew all about me, but then waffled on about power. I'd hoped she would tell me where I was born and who my real parents were, but she didn't really tell me anything at all."

"Well, maybe she didn't need to," he said, sitting me down

on the sofa before sitting down next to me. "I think I've found something out."

Excitement hit me once again. "You know?" I held my breath, hoping that the pieces would finally fit into place.

"Not exactly. Please don't get too excited yet. I managed to speak to someone who was a reporter around the time you were born. The whole kingdom was so excited to have a new princess, especially after the excitement of your parents' wedding, not to mention the waking of the princess and your grandparents. No one even thought to question where you came from or why you were adopted so soon after your parents married. They were only eighteen and nineteen years old. They had all the time in the world to have children of their own."

"Yeah, I know all that," I replied impatiently. "So, what else did he say?"

", it turns out our reporter friend was new to the job. He was young and eager to please. He thought the whole thing was suspicious. He went to the editor of the newspaper and said that he wanted to find out exactly who you were, but he was shot down."

"Why?" I asked appalled.

Milo shifted on the seat. "Apparently, the editor didn't want him snooping around and spoiling it. He said that the kingdom had seen enough sorrow, and he didn't want the reporter to bring the people down. The people only wanted good news, and the good news was selling papers. Thankfully for us, the reporter decided to go and investigate on his own."

"So, what did he find?" I jiggled impatiently.

"He interviewed a great many people. He didn't go to the obvious places like you did. He never went to the orphanage. He spoke to those people who worked night shifts."

"Night shifts?" Now, I was really confused.

"Yeah. Apparently, you weren't at the castle one day, and then, you were the next. No one saw you being brought to the castle. No one saw your parents going to pick you up. It was like you suddenly appeared one night."

Everyone I'd spoken to about it said the same thing.

I clapped my hands together excitedly. "And so he spoke to people who might have seen me being brought into the castle. Genius."

"Exactly," confirmed Milo. "He said he interviewed more than two dozen people with no luck, but then he struck it lucky. An old man was out stealing apples from an orchard just beyond the gates of the castle on the night you arrived. He hid behind a tree as a carriage passed. He heard a baby crying inside. More than one baby."

"I already know that. Remy's former nanny told me that she heard another baby, too. I'm sorry I should have told you that part."

Milo waved it off. "That's not all. He said that he saw who was driving the carriage."

"Who?" I asked, my voice laced with anticipation.

"There were two of them. A young woman and an old woman in a cloak. He followed the carriage up to the castle and then peered through the portcullis.

"It was the old woman that brought you out of the carriage. The younger one stayed inside the carriage the whole time. She walked you to the front door and spoke to your mother and father. He couldn't hear what was said, but she spoke to your parents for about ten minutes before jumping back in the carriage and racing back through the castle gates. He caught a glimpse of the younger woman as they barreled past him. He said that she had tears streaming down her face."

"That was all?"

"Yes. That's all. The old man has since died, and it was never printed. I'm sorry I couldn't find out more."

I kissed him lightly on the cheek. "You found out everything. You found out that my real mother didn't want to let me go. She loved me."

He wrapped his arms around me and brought me into a hug as tears began to fall down my face. "Actually, there was one more thing. He said the carriage looked like one of those from Urbis."

17TH JANUARY

I awoke to an urgent rapping on my door.

"Who is it?" I yelled out from under my covers.

"It's me."Oh, crap. Caspian.

"I think we should spend some time today working on our wedding," he shouted back through my bedroom door. "We didn't get nearly enough done the other day."

I rolled my eyes and dragged myself out of bed, wrapping my robe around myself.

"*The* wedding," I said, opening the door to him. "Not our wedding. There have been thousands of applicants for the position of my husband. Any one of them could win."

Caspian sneered and waved his hand dismissively. "Just a formality. I am the best swordsman there is, and beyond the guards at your castle, the people of Draconis aren't known for their fighting skills."

"Maybe, maybe not, but I wouldn't count your wedding favors just yet. I can't work with you on the wedding." I made to close the door on him, but he slipped his foot between the door and the frame. "I have to plan the competition," I reminded him.

"I don't know why you are bothering," he said. "It seems like a total waste of time, but if you must. I'll ask that lovely maid of yours to help me."

"Go ahead." Dahlia would probably love the idea of spending another day planning a wedding with Caspian, and if it kept the pair of them out of my hair, then all the better.

Kicking his foot back, I slammed the door, not wanting to speak to Caspian a moment longer. I had too much running through my mind, and I'd made it very clear that I didn't care one jot what the wedding was like. I didn't care about the dress, flowers, food. None of it. How could I even begin to care about any of that stuff when I didn't even care for my husband-to-be? Heck, I didn't even know who my husband-to-be was.

Dressing quickly, I made the decision to go to the library. I had the competition to plan, and that was much more important than the wedding. I needed to make it in such a way that Caspian didn't win.

Plus , at the back of my mind, I knew that all of this would be for nothing. The competition, the wedding, all of it. I would plan it like the dutiful princess I was, but I wouldn't be here to see it.

I was going to go to Urbis. After hearing that I might have been born there, it was the only possible lead I had, and I'd never forgive myself if I didn't go and check it out. I couldn't ask my father's permission. There was no way in this kingdom; he would let me travel alone to Urbis. I could have asked to bring Milo with me, but my father was already suspicious of him. No, I had to do this alone, and I had to do it without anyone knowing. The castle was going to be full of reporters next week. All here to write about and take pictures of the competition and the preparations leading up to it. Preparations that had not yet started.

If I handed my father a full list of what I planned to do for the competition, then he would not suspect anything. I hated leaving him, especially with my mother the way she was, but I was doing nothing here to help. I couldn't wake her up any more than the constant stream of doctors that saw her every day.

But...if all this really did have something to do with where I came from, then it was my duty to find out what. And if I could find a way to save my mother and maybe find my real mother at the same time, then fantastic.

Remy was already in the library, absorbed in his adventure books, as usual. He grinned at me when he saw me walk in and waved a book at me. I had to sit and read with him before doing anything. He wouldn't leave me alone for a second if I didn't. Half an hour later, when I'd read a few chapters of a book about the pirates of Skyla, and he'd acted out the swashbuckling parts with much glee, I finally pried myself away and found the book where Remy had originally found the information on the competition. The book, named *Winning the Legend* was so old that the leather binding it was beginning to crack, and the gold lettering on the spine had faded to almost nothing.

I opened it, flicking carefully to the page that mentioned the competition. It was so vague. It seemed there needed to be three parts. Part one had to be a game of skill, part two had to be a game of logic, and part three had to be a sword fight to the death.

Pulling a pencil and paper to myself, I wrote swordfight to the death in capitals.

I wondered how that would go down? If we killed all the men who had applied, we'd look like barbarians. It would make things easy for me, but I figured I should come up with something a little better. I didn't really want anyone to die on my behalf.

Milo would have been a good person to help me with

this, but he was working today, and Jack wouldn't be too pleased if he dashed off with me again. There was no way I'd be able to take him away from his post without Jack tattle-telling to my father. And, of course, my father wouldn't be too happy about one of the contestants helping me. No, I was in this on my own, whether I liked it or not

Part one. A game of skill. But what skill? Nothing Caspian was good at, that was for sure. I could rule magic out then. I should also stipulate in the rules that anyone caught using magic would be disqualified for cheating.

I thought of Milo and his strengths. He was a good swordsman, and no matter what Caspian said about the men of Draconis, I wouldn't want to count him out. He could rival Caspian with his sword skills, but could he beat him? I sighed. I just didn't know. Caspian could still beat me in a swordfight, something that irked me no end. Anyway, swordfighting was the final part of the competition. The first part had to be something else.

I thought about the sword that Milo had made me. It was beautiful. I couldn't ask the competitors to make swords, it would take too long, and we'd need so much metal and way too many tools, but what if we had them make something out of clay? It wasn't exactly Milo's area of expertise, but he was artistic and could turn his hand to anything. Caspian, on the other hand, had made nothing but trouble since being here. And piles of clay could easily be brought in. The makers of the best statues or pots would qualify for the next round. As I wrote pot in my notebook, a thought occurred to me. I gave a giggle and erased the word pot and added the word princess. If they were fighting for me, they could make me. They could design a figurine that looked like me. The ten closest ones would get through. That would certainly whittle the pool down.

Chewing a hangnail, I moved to the next part. Logic. I

probably should come up with some really clever logic puzzle, but I wasn't particularly good at them, and if I couldn't come up with anything clever, how would I expect others not to know the answer straight away?

I sat back in my chair, watching Remy. He was soundlessly acting out a part in his book, a sly smile on his face as he thrust his hand forward, killing some imaginary foe. When all this was over, I was going to take him to Skyla. The stories of pirates he read about were fiction, but I'd heard reports of pirates really sailing the waters around there. Not that I wanted him to actually meet a pirate, but he would be thrilled to just see the place where they lived. Part of Draconis bordered the ocean, but mountain ranges made it almost impossible to reach. We had no pretty sandy beaches that some of the other kingdoms boasted, and seaside villages on the Draconis coast were few and far between.

I decided to leave that part and move to the final part. A battle of swords. There was no way I was going to do that. I couldn't have someone's blood on my hands. Besides, as Caspian kept boasting, Swordfighting was one of his greatest skills. Pondering my other options for a second, I wrote down the word wrestling. Still not ideal, but the competition must have some form of combat, and wrestling was the safest I could think of beyond thumb wars, but my father would never go for that.

After another ten minutes of thinking, I wrote the word question under part two and left it at that. My father could come up with some crippling brain teaser. He was better at that sort of thing than I was.

Taking the paper out of the library, I headed down to my father's office. He sat quietly, a stack of papers on his desk, black circles under his eyes.

"What is it, Azia?" He sighed, his voice weary.

"I've finished planning the competition, Father." I handed

over the scrap of paper I'd written on. He took it and looked at it, reading it quickly before turning it over to look at the back as though there would be something more written.

"Is this it?"

I nodded.

"Part two says answer a clever question."

"That's right."

He handed me back the piece of paper. "Please stop playing games and take this seriously," he admonished, massaging his temples. "This is your doing, and you need to be the one to sort it out. I have enough going on without having to worry about this competition."

I bowed my head. "I'm sorry, Father. I'll do better. What is it you are working on? Maybe I can be of help."

He shook his head. "You'll help by sorting that out," he said, pointing to the paper he'd just given back to me. I'm in the process of bringing the best doctors in all the kingdoms here to look at your mother. It's not as easy as you'd think. Plus, that wall has become a bugbear. A lot of our people want me to go and kill the dragons instead of building a wall, and so, I've got people feuding, my own staff turning against me. Jacob is practically threatening to start a revolution over it. The whole thing is an utter nightmare."

I jumped on his words. The last time I'd spoken to him about the dragons, he'd been adamant he was going to send his men up to attack. "You aren't going up the mountain, then?"

He shook his head slowly. "I want to. Killing the whole bloody lot of them will solve a huge problem. They've been nothing but a headache, but I need my men in case something else happens. A lot of them are still out looking for spindles, another bloody waste of time. As long as the dragons stay up there, I'll leave them alone. If there is another episode like the one last week, I'll have them up there in a shot. My whole army. Jacob keeps on at me to do it. He's not happy spending his days building a wall."

This Jacob character was really beginning to irk me, but at least, it meant I could breathe easy about the dragons now. Vasuki promised to keep his dragons under control, and my father wouldn't attack unless they did. One headache resolved. Now, if only I could resolve the other million problems I had.

I bade my father farewell and headed back to the entrance hall. A huge weight had been lifted from my mind. A weight I didn't know I'd felt so heavily. I shouldn't care about the dragons as much as I did. I barely knew them, but Vasuki had been right when he said we shared an affinity. There was something about them that called to me, and for whatever reason, they had made me their queen. I felt it, too. My magic only worked around them. I'd tried a hundred times to perform magic in their absence, but nothing had worked, despite Caspian telling me how powerful I was.

"Ah, there you are..."

I swear that man could read minds.

"Hello, Caspian. I already told you that I can't help you with wedding stuff. Do whatever you want. I don't care anyway," I said, walking past him quickly.

I waved my hand dismissively in his direction as I passed, hoping he'd get the hint that I didn't care to speak to him about the wedding or anything else, but in his usual Caspian fashion, he didn't.

"Actually, I wasn't here for that," he said, skirting around to face me. "My friend is coming, and I'd like to make sure she is welcomed nicely."

"Excuse me?" I stopped and raised my eyebrows.

"Well, you do have an awful attitude about you most of the time, and that sour face is enough to turn anyone off. Not me. I find it rather hot when you scowl, but I'd like it if you could be a bit nicer to her."

I planted on a smile to hide my anger and clenched my fists tightly by my side.

Through gritted teeth, I spoke. "I meant, what are you doing, bringing your friends here? This isn't your castle, and may I remind you that you are a guest here... an unwelcome one?"

"Fine!" he said, turning on his heel. "I'll send Charlotte back to Urbis after her three-day trip to get here.Only I thought you'd want to speak to her as she is renowned on the subject of Morpheus."

He began to walk away, knowing full well I would call him back. "The friend you told me about?" I shouted at him a little louder than I intended. My voice echoed around the entrance hall.

He turned. "That is the one. If you don't mind, I'll borrow a horse to ride into Zhore to the Urbis Express station and tell her myself that she isn't wanted. I think she'll be a little peeved. After all, she only came here to help you, but we all know how your wishes come before anyone else's."

"Okay, I'm sorry," I said, a little quieter this time. "I'd love to meet her. I'll come with you to Zhore, and I'll get the kitchen staff to make her a welcome meal."

"That's what I thought," Caspian said, his sly grin returning to his face. "I'll meet you in the stables in ten minutes. Hurry up, though, I wouldn't want to have to set off without you."

I fumed all the way to the kitchen. Caspian was becoming more insufferable by the second, but I needed to see his friend. I wanted to know if Caspian had been telling me the truth or if it was just some elaborate scheme to be able to stay in the castle. He was having it easy here. I don't know what his life was like in The Forge, but he had a cushy existence here. Not that I could say much. I lived this way, but this was my home.

Ten minutes later, we were saddled up and ready to go. The snow was really coming down again, and the dreary skies matched my mood well. I barely spoke to Caspian as we trotted down the road, but despite my murderous feelings toward him, I felt a flutter of excitement...no hope, in meeting this friend of his. I wasn't convinced that he was telling me the truth. I could never tell with him, but if this woman proved to be trustworthy and knowledgeable, then there was a chance...a slim chance I would be able to find Morpheus and the entrance to the dream world. If I could do that, I'd be able to find my mother and free her from her mental prison. My father had only just told me he was bringing in the best doctors from all the lands, but I already knew that it was a pointless endeavor. I think he knew that, too, but he felt as powerless as I did. If finding doctors helped him get through this, then I was all for it. Maybe they would be able to help him if not my mother.

I'd only ever seen the Urbis Express from a distance. When we traveled for royal visits, we only took the royal train, or sometimes, if it wasn't too far away like Badalah, we took horses and a carriage. I'd often looked to the skies and seen the large airships flying overhead and wished I was on them. It must be so wonderful to be able to fly above the kingdom in the comfort of a seat rather than in the talons or on the back of a dragon.

The huge airship was already in dock, and people were beginning to disembark. Despite the massive proportions of the ship, the part that held people was actually very small, only holding up to twenty passengers plus four crew members at a time. It made it an extremely expensive way to travel, which only the elite could afford. My family could afford it. Indeed, there was a special section on every Urbis express reserved for royalty and high-up dignitaries, but my mother was scared of heights, so we never used it.

I scanned the people heading towards us as Caspian jumped down from his horse. I was looking for an incredibly attractive fae, so I was surprised when the woman he hugged was human and average looking. Her medium brown hair was tied back, and she wore no makeup. Her clothes were smart like a business woman might wear, and nothing like the over-the-top attire that Caspian chose to wear on a daily basis.

I jumped down from my horse as Caspian brought her over.

"I'm very privileged to meet you, Your Highness," she said, dropping into a low curtsey.

"Oh, don't bother with all that, Charlotte," he said airily. "It's only, Azia. She doesn't need bowing down to."

Charlotte's eyes opened wide, and her bushy eyebrows shot up under her messy bangs.

"It's okay," I said, holding out my hand for her to shake and kicking Caspian's calf at the same time with my boot. "Caspian is right. We have no need of formalities here. We are all friends."

"Well, I'm very excited to meet you," she said, giving me a shy smile. "I couldn't believe it when Caspian told me you wanted to meet me. I never thought my degree would come in useful. My parents thought I was silly to take it, but look at me now. Heading to the Draconis Castle with the princess herself. That'll show my parents, eh?"

I laughed at her enthusiasm. Despite my reservations at her being Caspian's friend, I liked her a great deal already. A lot more than I liked Caspian, but then again, that wasn't saying much.

Caspian helped her onto the back of his horse, and the three of us made our way back to the castle.

Charlotte's mouth dropped as I escorted her into the castle. She gazed about her as I took her coat, her eyes drifting from place to place as she took it all in.

"It's so beautiful," she murmured.

"It's home, and you are very welcome here," I said. "I've had some food put out for you. Are you hungry?"

She nodded enthusiastically. "I'm famished. I couldn't afford to buy much food on the Urbis Express. I've only eaten a couple of sandwiches and some apples for the past few days."

"I've had a room made up for you. If you want to put your bags in there and then come back down to lunch."

She grinned and gave me the thumbs up as I asked a maid to take her to her guest room.

Caspian and I sat in the small dining room, waiting for her.

"Charlotte seems nice," I said, absently. The food had already been brought out buffet style, and the smell was causing my stomach to jump. I'd not realized how hungry I was.

"She's very knowledgeable. Anything you want to know about Morpheus, she will be able to tell you."

"How do you know her?"I asked genuinely interested. She didn't seem like someone Caspian would spend time with.

"I spent some time in Urbis a few years back, and we met then. I liked the fact that she was different from the girls at The Forge."

"I remember you saying the same thing about me once." I grinned, picking up a carrot stick and taking a bite.

"You are nothing like Charlotte," he said. I didn't have time to question him on what he meant because Charlotte chose that moment to walk through the door. She'd changed into a pretty but understated pink dress, and her hair was now down. She was a bonny girl with a sweet face that had an innocence about it.

"This looks yummy," she stated, taking in the spread of food.

I watched her as she ate. She took little bites out of everything, almost like a squirrel would. Every time Caspian spoke, her eyes would dart over to him.

"Charlotte took a course in the Gods at Urbis University, but Morpheus was her specialty. She knows more about Morpheus than anyone," Caspian said. At this, Charlotte's face lit up like a beacon.

"Not really," she said, smiling shyly. "I'm sure there are other people who know more than I."

"I doubt it."

Charlotte positively beamed at his words.

"So," she said, talking to me. "Caspian tells me you want to know about Morpheus. He's already told me your situation."

"Do you think you'll be able to help me?" I asked.

"I'm not a mage. All I can do is tell you what I know."

"Which is a lot," said Caspian

"Which is a lot when it comes to Morpheus," she said.

I was eager to hear what she had to say. Anything that could help my mother.

Before she spoke, the door to the dining room opened. "Have you finished the competition yet?"

I looked to the door to where my father stood. His eyes bulged from lack of sleep, and his hair stuck up at all angles. He looked crazed.

"Not yet, Father, but..."

"I've just had a messenger from the Sentinel up at the castle again. I promised it to them yesterday."

"But Father..."

"But father, nothing. You promised me this morning that you'd get it done, and here I find you having a tea party. I'm going to bed. I've not slept for thirty-six hours straight. I need this done by the time the paper goes to press. They gave me a deadline of five o'clock."

Without another word, he slammed the door behind him as he left. A glance at the clock told me I had a little under two hours to come up with three parts to this stupid competition. If only he'd listened to me about Charlotte and why she was here, he would have slept more soundly, but I didn't have the heart to go running after him. If he was going to bed, it was kinder to leave him be.

"I should go and do what he wants. I've been putting it off," I explained. "I'm so sorry, Charlotte."

"Would you like me to help you?" Caspian asked.

"No. Why don't you take Charlotte for a tour of the castle grounds? The weather's cleared up a little."

"Oh , yes, please," she said, practically bouncing out of her seat."I'd love to."

I left them both with a smile on my face. Charlotte's crush on Caspian was obvious. Insane, but obvious. Her eyes barely left him the whole lunchtime. He, on the other hand, hardly looked at her at all.

I really hated the fact I had to wait to hear what she had to say about Morpheus. I don't know what scared me the most. My mother being in a coma, her being cursed, or her being locked in a dream realm by some crazy god, but if I knew what it was, it would bring me closer to being able to deal with it.

I went to the library expecting to find Remy there. It was quiet, but his books still lay on the floor where he'd left them. I picked them all up and shelved them, before opening the cabinet with the special books in it and pulling the one with the contest in it out.

After reading it for what felt like three hundred times, I sat back in the chair and closed my eyes. This was too hard.

I looked at the piece of paper I'd scribbled on earlier. The clay thing was a good idea, and the fighting seemed to be mandatory, whether I liked it or not.

I just needed a question that Caspian would never be able to answer, a question that Milo would jump on. Nothing too obvious. Not that it really mattered as I was planning on not being here anyway, but if it did get postponed and I did get forced to go through it at some later date.

And then it came to me. With a grin on my face, I wrote it down.

"What is the name of the Queen of Dragons?"

18TH JANUARY

Charlotte was already sitting at the table when I came down for breakfast. She sat up in her chair and gave me a bright, breezy smile.

"I'm so glad you are here. One of your staff members woke me up and told me that breakfast was served, but I thought that I'd come to the wrong place when there was no one here."

"It will get very noisy soon. Just wait and see. I have three brothers who love food. In fact, I'd eat now before they come down and eat it all... Caspian thinks that my mother's curse is actually something to do with Morpheus," I said, trying to bring the subject around to the reason she was here.

"From what Caspian tells me, it possibly is the case. I'd have to see her, of course, but if it's like the curse she was under before, then I'd say Morpheus has a hand in it."

"How do you know Morpheus had anything to do with the curse before?" I asked. "A witch called Derillen performed the spell originally. I think it's Derillen again this time."

The door opened, and Caspian walked in.

"Azia thinks a lot of things," Caspian explained to Charlotte, "but she's very rarely correct."

Charlotte pushed his arm. "You are such a monster. Don't be so rude."

"Yeah, Caspian. Don't be so rude."

"You love it!" he said, swiveling his eyes to me.

"I'd agree with you if you were right," I snapped back.

"Let's assume it's the same person doing this..." Charlotte said, steering us back to the original topic of conversation.

"It's not," butted in Caspian.

"We'll let's, for the sake of argument, say it is," Charlotte continued. "I don't know much about what happened to your mother back then. It's a little before my time. I was only five when she woke up. I did write about her in my dissertation, but I didn't cover much. My hypothesis was that Derillen had somehow become friendly with Morpheus, and Morpheus had closed the entrances to the dream world for your mother. Other people could enter and leave, but your mother was lost."

"You see, that's the part I don't understand. How come other people could come and go, and my mother couldn't. Why couldn't she go with them."

"it's not that simple. We all have our own exit and entrance. We get there through dreaming. If we didn't, we'd wake up after a nap in someone else's head. It is possible...nay, probable that your mother is seeing these other people. If you've dreamed about your mother, it's possible that you have actually seen her, but like most dreams, we wake up and forget straight away. Occasionally, we remember our dreams, but usually they are strange. That's the dream world. It is a strange place. Morpheus likes to confuse."

"So, if I dreamed about my mother, I could talk to her?"

Charlotte shrugged. "It's possible she will see you and be

able to talk to you. You might have already even been speaking to her every night, but unless you remember the dream, you wouldn't even know it."

My mind was blown by the thought of it. If Charlotte's hypothesis was right, I could spend my nights speaking to any number of people and not even know. It was a strange thought and one that didn't sit well in my stomach. I grabbed a sandwich and bit into it, chewing as I considered the implications of it.

"If you remember the story, your mother's curse was to kill her not to make her sleep. Derillen gave her the curse when she was a baby, but it didn't come into effect until she was seventeen years old. That gave your grandparents plenty of time to find other people of magic to stop the curse. The problem was that once a curse is given, only the original curse giver can break it."

I sat forward, intrigued. She knew more about my mother than I did. I'd not really been told this part of the story, just the bit about her waking up.

"Your mother was sent into hiding for the first part of her life, even though many people of magic told your grandfather that no amount of hiding could keep her from the curse. He didn't believe them, or he didn't want to believe them, so your mother barely saw her own parents throughout her childhood. Meanwhile, your grandfather hired every mage he could get his hands on. At one time, believe it or not, Draconis was the most magical kingdom, even beating out Enchantia, where most of the population is magic to some extent. "

She took a pause as she sipped on her tea. "There was almost an explosion of magic, but even then, they couldn't stop the curse, only lessen it. They made the curse so that if your mother pricked her finger, she would only fall asleep, not die."

"Which she did."

"Yes, but they made it so she would only fall asleep for one night. She was supposed to wake up the next day with nothing more wrong with her than a sore finger."

"How do you know all this?" I exclaimed.

"I told you. I used your mother's story as part of my dissertation. I spent four years studying Morpheus, and your mother's story is one of the more fascinating parts of my research."

"So where does he come in?"

"Well, " she said, clapping her hands together, "Derillen knew she had been beaten. The curse would still happen, but it would barely affect your mother at all. She was angry, but against so many people of magic, even she, with all her power, could do nothing. Nor dare she do any more curses with all the mages and fae looking after the young princess. But our Derillen was cunning. She knew a way around it. She somehow got to Morpheus, and between them, they cooked up the plan to close your mother's exit."

"How did she find Morpheus?" I asked.

Charlotte shrugged and rolled her eyes at the same time." That's where it gets difficult. I don't know how she found him. The gods don't live on the mortal realm. They do visit from time to time, but they spend most of the time wherever it is that gods live. There is no way to get there. Only the gods themselves can come and go. There have been many reports of people meeting the gods throughout the ages, but Morpheus is a slippery character. He is a master of disguise and can shift himself into any shape. I could be Morpheus, and you'd never know. Caspian could be him."

"I'd make a great god," he said, putting his hands behind his head.

Ignoring him, I asked Charlotte another question. "If he is so hard to find, how did Derillen do it?"

"I don't know. I've never been able to find out. She was a very powerful witch, which might have helped. Morpheus is drawn to power. If she went looking for him, there is a chance he heard about her and made himself known to her."

"Could we find him? I mean, is there a chance I could find him?"

She shrugged again? "I don't want to give you any false illusions. You will be very lucky if you do find him. Even then, you'll have to have something he wants in exchange. He won't open the portal to the dream world for just anybody."

"Is there a way for us to find this portal without him?"

"No," Charlotte answered, shaking her head. "It's not in a fixed place. Morpheus conjures it up when he wants to visit the dream world and when he's done, the portal disappears. It could be anywhere, and it's only open when he's in the mortal realm. If he decides to spend the next fifty years in the realm of the gods, we'll never be able to find him."

The whole thing seemed impossible, but there was no other hope for my mother. No medic or healer would be able to help her. It was either find the witch that cursed her or find Morpheus to unblock her way back. As I had no clue where to start finding either of them, the whole thing seemed pointless.

"So, I should give up."

"You do have more pressing matters," Caspian cut in. "Namely, your wedding to plan."

I noticed Charlotte slump as he mentioned the wedding.

"I've never met him, and believe me, I've looked. That's why I moved to Urbis in the first place. The sightings of him have always been there. He doesn't seem to travel to other kingdoms. If you are going to find him, Urbis is the place to be, but like I said, I've spent four years looking for him, and I've never met him...or at least I don't know that I have. There is a chance I met him and didn't know it."

She must have seen my crestfallen face.

"Look. You are prettier than I'll ever be, and that will give you the upper hand. He likes beautiful women."

She was putting herself down. She was pretty, just in an understated way. I watched as she slid her eyes to Caspian in the hope he'd contradict her on her level of beauty. Of course, he didn't. He was happy to talk about how clever she was, but he was blind to her. Idiot.

"I'm not sure I like the idea of you going to find him if that's the case," he said. "You are mine, and I'm not about to share you with some god."

Double idiot!

"I'm not yours," I reminded him, seeing the stricken look on Charlotte's face. "I've never been yours, and I'll never be yours."

"You will if I win the competition."

"If you'll excuse me." Charlotte stood up quickly, her face turned away from Caspian so he couldn't see her tears. "I've eaten a little too much. I think I should go lie down for a bit. Thank you for the food. It was lovely."

She dashed out of the door so quickly, I didn't have time to stop her.

"She barely ate anything," Caspian commented.

I glared at him. "You really are stupid, you know that?"

He sat up in his chair, giving me a what-did-I-do look.

I dashed out the door up to the room I'd had made up for Charlotte. I knocked on the door, but I could hear her sobbing quietly inside.

"It's me," I shouted through. A few seconds later, the door opened a crack. Before she had chance to speak, I said what I wanted to say.

"He's an ass. You know that, right?"

She opened the door a little more and let me come in.

"I'm sorry I ran like that. He's not the idiot. I am. I've been in love with him since the second I met him."

"I hate to break this to you, Charlotte, but he's easily the most awful person I've ever met."

"He doesn't think that about you," she said sadly, sitting back down on the bed.

"He's an obnoxious creep. Why on earth do you like him?"

"He's weird around you," she said. "He's not normally like this. Yeah, he's always been full of himself, but look how gorgeous he is. He's perfect."

Moving on...

"Weird how?" He was weird to me all the time, so I didn't know any different.

"He's not so cocky with you."

I laughed so hard I almost fell off the bed. "If this is him not being cocky, I'd hate to see him usually."

"He really likes you. The way he's acting is just for show. I've never seen him like this. He's always been cocky, but I've never seen him be rude before. I met him in my freshman year in a bar in Urbis. I was drawn to him right away. I'm not really a bar dweller, but I was out looking for Morpheus. As soon as Caspian walked in, he was surrounded by women trying to get his attention. I thought at the time he might be Morpheus. He has the same traits. Beautiful, confidant. When Caspian got annoyed at the constant attention-seeking, he slipped out the back. I followed him and let him hide in my apartment. "

"Uh, huh."

"It wasn't like that...okay, maybe it was. I was no better than those other girls, I wanted him just as much, but I guess I was cleverer."

"I still can't get over him having a swarm of girls after him," I said.

"He's popular in Urbis... He's popular everywhere, really."

"Not around here, he's not."

She gave a wry smile. "I think you are the only girl that hasn't fallen for his charms, which is ironic, really."

"I'm yet to see any charms. He's tried to kill me twice."

"I doubt that. This is the first time I've seen him actually like someone."

She sounded sad. "I don't see what you are seeing. He treats me awfully. I admit he can be nice sometimes, but he usually messes it up."

"He wouldn't be this insistent on marrying you if he didn't want to."

"I thought he wanted to marry me because he wanted power."

Charlotte shook her head. "Do you even know who he is?"

Now it was my turn to shake my head. "What do you mean?"

"He is a member of the Urbis government. He's the president of magic and magical beings. Basically, any laws pertaining to magic have to be signed off by him before they can become laws. He might not be a member of royalty like you, but in some regards, he's already more powerful politically than you'll ever be.'

My mind reeled with this new information. Caspian served in the Urbis government. Charlotte was right when she said he had a lot of power. Even my parents had told me he was powerful, but I thought they meant magically. The leaders of each kingdom were governed by the government in Urbis. Mostly, Urbis left the eleven kingdoms to their own devices, but sometimes, they waded in when they felt something wasn't being done right. He was giving up a lot to be here with me.

"It doesn't matter. I dislike the man so much that I opened up a competition to all the men in Draconis to marry me. It was either that or marry Caspian."

She giggled at this. "I bet that didn't go down too well."

"Not at all. He hates it, but tough. I don't want to marry him."

"I'd do anything to be like you. You really are beautiful. It's no wonder he likes you. I've known him for four years, and I don't think he's even noticed I'm a woman."

I looked down at my clothes. I was happiest in my scruffy clothes so I could go out and practice fighting, but Dahlia usually managed to make me half decent every morning, whether I liked it or not. Today, she'd put me in a pretty blouse and skirt combo. She'd even managed to do something with my hair.

I looked closely at Charlotte.

"I think I can help you. You need some Dahlia treatment."

"What's that?" she asked, eyes wide.

"You'll see, but first of all, tell me more about Morpheus."

"Like I told you before, I've never seen him, but if you want to find your mother, finding him is the only way. You'll have to be clever, and you'll have to seduce him. You'll also have to go to Urbis. He's not once been spotted outside of the city."

I nodded. I'd already made my mind up to go to Urbis. I was born there, or at least I think I was. It was like everything was coming together, and the path I needed to take was an obvious one.

"If you do decide to come to Urbis, you are very welcome to stay with me. My apartment is small, but I have a spare bed. It's the least I can do after your hospitality."

"Thank you. I might have to take you up on that. How do you know all this? I mean, how do you know that the dream world exists, and how do you know that Derillen found Morpheus and got him to close my mother's exits?"

"I know of Morpheus because I dreamed about him once. I've always had lucid dreams, which makes me more susceptible to him. He came to me when I was in the dream world. He was so beautiful, I knew right then I wanted him . He told me his name, but then he left me alone. I woke up completely in love. I'm not a religious person, but I'd heard about the god Morpheus. It was then, I decided to learn more about him at university. There have been many sightings of him over the years. Some, I'm not sure are true; but some, I believe.

"As for Derillen, I stumbled upon her story in my second year. As I was researching Morpheus, I looked for any articles that were about sleep. The fact that Derillen had the ability to stop your mother waking up was what made me know that Morpheus was involved. No one is more powerful than the gods. Not fae, not mages, not even witches. The gods are about as powerful as you can get, so if anyone was stopping your mother from waking up, I knew it was him."

"Do you have concrete proof?"

She shook her head. "No, but I know everything there is to know about sleep, and there are only two ways to stop someone waking up. Either kill them or lock them in the dream realm. If your mother is still breathing, it has to be the latter, and if it's the latter, it means Morpheus is involved. There is no other explanation."

I tried to think around her reasoning. "What about illness? People in comas don't wake up."

"People in comas don't wake after a hundred-year sleep, not having aged a day either."

True," I conceded, "but could it be that she is in a coma now?"

"I don't know for sure, but Caspian told me that your father has had her looked at by many doctors, and they all agree there is nothing wrong with her. If there is nothing wrong with her, then she's trapped. There's one way to tell for sure."

"There is?" I wanted to believe her so badly, but I was the type of person that needed proof rather than guesswork. Even four years of study wasn't enough unless I could see it with my own eyes.

"I'd need to see her, and then, I can tell you if it's a coma or not."

The maid was by my mother's bed as I entered her room. She held a book in her hand as she had the last time I'd been to visit.

"I've been reading to her," she explained. "I thought maybe if she could hear a soothing voice, she might respond to it, you know."

"Thank you," I said, giving her a warm smile. Behind me, Charlotte whispered that a freight train could go through the room, and my mother wouldn't hear it.

The maid gave Charlotte a funny look as she walked around us to leave the room. No doubt she'd go straight to my father to tell him that I was here with a strange woman, not that it mattered. By the time my father came up the stairs to find out what was going on, we'd already know what was wrong with her.

"My father has hired the best physicians and healers in all the land. They'll all be arriving soon. The castle will be full again."I took my mother's hand. It was so cold.

"Just like your grandfather did all those years ago with the mages and fae, not that all the people of magic in the world would be able to help her if I'm right." She looked me in the eye. "I hope I'm wrong and that this is something else. Then those healers will be able to help her."

"I hope so too," I said. "So what do we need to do to tell if she's in a coma? Some kind of spell?"

Charlotte gave a small mirthless laugh. "I'm not magic. I'm originally from Arcadia, and there are not many people of magic there. No. This is something much more simple. If she is in a coma and you pull back her eyelids, you'll see her pupils. Most coma patients don't react to light. Some do."

"So what happens if she isn't in a coma? If she's cursed?"

Charlotte leaned over my mother and gently put her thumbs on her eyelids. "If she's in the Dream Realm, she'll not have any pupils at all." She pulled back her eyelids.

I looked down. Pain gripped my chest as my worse fear was realized. All I saw were the whites of her eyes. My mother was definitely cursed.

19TH JANUARY

"Dahlia asked me to tell you that there is a reporter from the Sentinel waiting to speak with you," Milo said after my good morning kiss. "Oh, and she said to dress up nicely...her version of nicely, not yours. She said they are waiting in the main hall, so hurry up."

"Urgh!" I sighed as I opened my wardrobe and pulled out a dress. I had too much going on to care about reporters. I had a trip to Urbis to plan. There were way too many reasons for me to go there now. I needed to find out who I was, but I also had to save my mother from Morpheus's clutches. The only way I was going to get close to doing any of those was to travel to Urbis.

I'd sent the three parts of the competition to the Sentinel by way of one of the castle staff a couple of days before, so I expected that was the reason they wanted to see me. I'd also done it without showing my father first. I didn't want to give him any more reason to make me do the whole thing again. I had too much on my plate to worry about a competition that I had no intention of holding, and my father was equally as busy. I was doing him a favor, really.

"I'll leave you to it," Milo smiled, "But maybe we could do some more sword practice when my shift ends?"

"Sure thing," I replied as he shut my bedroom door behind him.

I pulled out a beige dress that matched my mood perfectly and pulled it over my head. After running a brush through my hair and tying it back with a ribbon, I was ready to face whatever the Sentinel reporter had to throw at me. He'd no doubt want a couple of pictures, and for that, I should have put on some makeup, but I just wanted to get the whole thing over and done with as quickly as possible. I needed the time to plan my trip before I went out with Milo. I couldn't ask for his help because I wasn't planning on telling him I was going. He'd only try and stop me. The only person I was planning on telling was Nyre because I was planning on taking her with me. I'd be spotted if I tried getting to Urbis on the Urbis Express or on the train, which left me with three options. Walk, go on horseback or fly, courtesy of my little dragon friend. Nyre was the quickest option.

The main hall was packed with people, all of which turned their eyes to me as I entered.

"What's going on now?" I whispered to myself as I walked between the men, for they were almost all men. The only woman in the whole room was Dahlia, who bustled towards me when I walked through the door.

"What's going on?" I asked, though I was sure I didn't really want to know.

"Didn't Milo tell you? The Sentinel people are here. They want to do a feature as a way to build up excitement for the competition next week."

"You're telling me they sent this many reporters?" I asked as she hustled me up to the raised throne area.

"Don't be silly. The two in the front row are the Sentinel reporter and photographer."

"So, who are the others?" I asked, gazing over the heads of all the men. There were so many of them. Hundreds.

"They are the people we've selected for the competition. We invited them here today to meet you before they compete for you."

"Oh, you did, did you?" I asked weakly. So much for planning my getaway. I wouldn't even be able to practice my sword fighting with Milo at this rate.

"It wasn't just me. It was the castle administration team."

"What did my father say about this?" I inquired, looking around the hall. He was nowhere to be seen. Neither was Caspian or Milo. I knew Milo was working, but I had no idea where Caspian was when all this was going on. Hopefully, asking Charlotte out on a date so I could cancel this whole thing. Dahlia shrugged and moved back without answering my question.

"I'll do a quick interview afterward," the Sentinel reporter piped up, "but first, we'd like to get some shots of you talking to your suitors."

"Great," I said, not doing a good job of hiding my sarcastic tone.

"Andrew, first!" Dahlia said as I sat down in my father's throne. It was the first time I'd ever sat in it, not that it brought me any joy to think about it. I'd prefer to be literally anywhere than right where I was.

"This is Andrew," Dahlia said, bringing a shy-looking boy up to me. He didn't look much older than me, and the way he kept his eyes down told me he was nervous about meeting me. You and me both, Buddy.

"Andrew is my son," Dahlia said proudly, giving me a wink and pointing to him. "He's perfect," she mouthed silently behind his back. I smirked. The poor kid looked like he was about to lose his lunch.

"Hi, Andrew. I've heard a lot about you," I lied. All I'd heard were complaints that he wasn't doing as well as he could be in school.

"Really?" he said. His voice was almost a whisper. I talked to him for an excruciating two minutes while the photographer snapped away. The poor guy could barely string a sentence together and replied to everything I said in monosyllables.

"He's just a little shy," Dahlia explained as she ushered him off the stage. "You'll need to go through the rest more quickly or we'll be here all day. Just a how do you do and on to the next." What followed was no better. In nine hundred men, I would have thought I'd like at least one of them, but between the oafs, the men who forgot to speak, the men that thought they already owned me, not to mention the man who asked when his coronation would be, I was thoroughly bored and annoyed by the time it came to eat. To my chagrin, all these men had been invited to eat, and tables full of sandwiches were brought in.

There was no escape for me. Every time I tried to leave, Dahlia was there, reminding me of my duty. In the end, I grabbed a sandwich and sat on the floor in the very back corner of the room behind my father's throne. It wasn't ideal, but at least, I was mostly shielded from view, and no one else was allowed up here, so I'd get a little peace before it would all start again in the afternoon.

A shadow loomed above me. I was all set to tell them where to go when I looked up and saw Caspian with a tray full of food and a couple of glasses of wine.

"I thought you might want a bit more than a soggy sandwich," he said, sitting down and putting the tray between us.

It was filled with fruit and pastries. My stomach grumbled at the sight of it.

"And I thought this might help you get through the afternoon," he said, handing me the wine. I took the glass from him and downed it in one go while he picked up a pastry for himself.

"You know, I never thought I'd say this, but you are looking quite the catch compared to the competition."

His mouth curled up at the edges in a picture of smugness.

"You brought this on yourself," he reminded me. "You could have had this." He indicated his body.

"You are hot," I agreed, probably because the wine was strong, and it had already gone to my head.

"There's still time. We could call this off. We could elope..."

"I could throw myself out of my bedroom window," I said, taking Caspian's wine and downing that too. If I was going to have to repeat this morning, I was going to do it drunk.

"I mean it. I could go and speak to your father right now. I know it's what he wants. He's sick of all this as much as you are."

He swept his head toward the rest of the hall, where nearly nine hundred men were eating.

"I suppose you can't be much worse than the guy whose feet smelled so bad that I almost threw up on him."

"Let's do it then," Caspian urged.

"You are forgetting one thing," I said, "You are a total ass, and I hate you."

"Hate is such a strong word," Caspian lamented, but the smile was still firmly on his gorgeous face. Urgh. Two glasses of wine, and my brain had completely given up.

"You are in love with that Milo chap, huh? Do you really think he can beat me?"

"He kicked your ass before," I reminded him of the time in his bedroom. "I see no reason why he won't be able to do it again. Besides. I'm not in love with him. I'm not in love with anyone. I just like him a lot. A lot more than you anyway."

"So you aren't in love with him? Well then, you won't mind if I do this." He leaned forward, and before I had time to react, he was kissing me. My mind was outraged, but my drunken brain wouldn't get my body to work quickly enough. My mind was saying move, but it felt so good, and the room spun around me.

Slap! Caspian brought his hand up to his cheek as I slapped him hard.

"How dare you!" I hissed, glaring at him.

"I notice it took you more than a few seconds to pull away," he remarked, grabbing another pastry. "And I didn't feel any resistance. In fact, I would say that you rather enjoyed it."

With that, he popped the pastry into his mouth, gave me a wink, and walked away, leaving me on my own, hiding behind my father's throne.

"Insufferable jerk!" I said loudly to no one in particular. The worst part was, he wasn't wrong. I had enjoyed it. I'd enjoyed it much more than I wanted to admit. Damn the fae!

He stood watching me all afternoon. Everywhere I looked, I could see him in the corner of my eye. His smart pale blue outfit stood out amongst the grays and blues and browns that the other men had elected to wear. I hated that I'd enjoyed kissing him, that it had been exciting, passionate, and forbidden, hidden behind my father's throne in a room with nine hundred men, all of which wanted to marry me. I couldn't even tell anyone about it either. If I told my father, he'd insist I marry the fae. If I even hinted that I'd kissed Caspian to Dahlia, she'd be ecstatic once she got over the fact I wasn't going to marry her beloved son. And I really couldn't tell Milo. Sweet, beautiful Milo, who didn't deserve this. I'd told him time and time again that I didn't want a boyfriend, all the while stringing him along, kissing him at every available opportunity. And I loved kissing Milo. It was a beautiful thing, and when our lips met, it was just right. Perfect. I was at home. But with Caspian, it had been full of raw danger, excitement, and a whole host of negative emotions that were currently swirly around my mind. My stomach did the same, thanks to the wine that I was most definitely not used to. I swear I was slurring my words by the time I'd managed to speak to all the men. After an extremely brief interview with the Sentinel reporter I hurried up to my room before anyone else could take more of my time. To my relief, Milo had already left for the day. He must have seen what was going on and realized I wasn't going to be able to put in any practice that day. I would have to tell Milo about the kiss. It was only fair, but I wasn't in any fit state to do it now. I yawned as I sat on my bed and tried to put my feelings together. It was no use. My feelings for Milo eclipsed anything I'd ever felt before, and yet I could still taste Caspian on my lips. I remembered clearly the feel of his lips on mine.

"Urgh," I cried out in frustration, falling back on my bed and pulling a pillow over my face.

I probably would have stayed that way all evening if it wasn't for the tapping on my window. Looking up, I saw Nyre outside.

I opened the window, and she hopped in quickly. A minute later, she was sitting on my bed in her transformed form as naked as the day she was born.

"Here," I said, throwing her a robe. She laughed as she pulled it around herself, covering her body with the soft downy night robe. She snuggled into it before looking up at me.

"You humans are so uptight. We don't wear clothes up on the mountain."

I made sure my bedroom door was closed as she paraded up and down in front of my mirror, gazing at herself in the robe. I'd have to throw her a pretty dress next time.

"That's as may be," I said, "but down here, we do, and if anyone was to walk in, they'd get quite a shock to see a naked woman on my bed."

"A naked dragon!" she stated but grinned at me, all the same.

"What can I do for you, Nyre?" I asked. The truth was, I was glad to see her. I didn't have any female friends, and beyond my mother and the female staff in the castle, I didn't know any other girls.

"Nothing. I thought I'd come down and see how you are holding up. My father has all the dragons on guard, ready for attack from your father. The plan is to make sure everyone is down in the settlement apart from the egg layers. Dragons have laid eggs in nests for generations because the altitude is good for them."

I sighed and sat on the bed. "I don't think my father is going to attack the dragons anymore. The people of Draconis want him to, but he's got a lot going on. He's trying to bring in the best doctors from the other kingdoms for my mother, and all his attention is there at the moment."

"Well, that's great news...Not about your mom, but about the doctors. Do you think they will help her?"

I shrugged my shoulders. "I don't think so. She isn't sick. She is cursed."

I told her about Derillen and Charlotte's theory of where my mother was. Just thinking about Charlotte brought back the guilt of kissing Caspian. She was completely besotted with him. Milo wouldn't be the only one upset by the kiss earlier. I finished my story and broke down in tears.

"No frowns, babe," Nyre said, bringing me into a hug. "Dragons don't cry."

"I'm not a dragon," I reminded her.

"No, you're the freaking Queen of the dragons! My father says so, and so it must be true."

I snorted a laugh as my tears dripped onto her shoulder, dampening the robe.

"I kissed an asshole."

"Ew." she crinkled her nose up, pulling away from me. "I hope you are not speaking literally because you know I'm not into that shit, right?"

I cracked up again, and the tears that had felt so real turned to tears of laughter.

"I was talking about a guy. The guy is an asshole."

"Ooh. " she sat forward, her hands clasped together, excitement about the change in topic coloring her features. "Which one? The fae? I know you're not talking about Milo. That guy is about as far from asshole as you can get."

I'd forgotten she'd seen me with Caspian once. The first time I'd used my magic, I'd been out with him, and the dragons had flown down out of the sky to bow down to me.

"That's the one," I said, nodding. "He kissed me today, and I feel like shit because of it. I'm not sure Milo will forgive me."

She weighed my words. "He's super hot, but if you say he's an asshole, then he's an asshole. Let's break this down, shall we? You say that he kissed you. Did you initiate it?"

I shook my head. "No. I didn't even want him to kiss me. I was a little tipsy."

"Well, there you have it," she said, clapping her hands together a little too excitedly. "You didn't want him to kiss you, and you were too drunk to fend him off."

She made it sound so cut and dried as though I wasn't somehow to blame for the mess I'd found myself in.

"Hmmm," I sighed. I wanted to believe her, but the fact remained I'd enjoyed it. Despite me hating Caspian, despite me wanting to shove a sword through his gut every time I spoke to him, I'd enjoyed kissing him.

"Urgh!" I said, throwing away the mental image. Every time I closed my eyes, there he was. "Let's not talk about him. There's something else I'd like to talk to you about. Actually, I'd like a favor from you. "

"Ooooh," she said, sitting up. "What is it? You want me to distract Milo while you secretly run to Caspian's room? I'll do it. Milo is cute, too." She threw me a wink.

"Keep your hands off Milo," I grumbled. "And no, that's definitely not it. I want to..."

Nyre jumped up off the bed as someone knocked on the door.

"Who is it?"

I'd not bolted the door. Whoever it was could walk in at any moment if they wanted. I waved my hand at Nyre to motion to her to hide. Dahlia wasn't known for waiting for an answer, and Caspian had been in my room uninvited a little too often to trust him to wait outside until I opened the door.

"It's me"

So it was Caspian. Beside me, Nyre jumped up and down in a little dance and clapped her hands together. I threw her a warning and pointed to the bathroom. She smirked as she left the room. I waited until she'd closed the bathroom door before opening the bedroom door to Caspian.

"What is it?" I asked, opening the door a crack.

"Can I come in?" He turned to look at the brute my father had hired to stand at the end of the corridor. Jack and Milo were obviously not working today.

"Nope."

"We can do this out in the corridor if you prefer. I'm sure

your father would love to hear our conversation about the kiss."

"Come in," I hissed, pulling him in and shutting the door behind him.

"There was no kiss," I said, not bothering to hide my irritation. "I want to forget it ever happened."

He moved close to me, his eyes boring into mine. "Oh, but it did happen. It happened, and you enjoyed it." The way he looked at me stirred something within me, and his magical energy radiated from him. An image blazed in my mind of his lips against mine as we illicitly hid behind my father's throne. The tingling from his energy centered on my lips causing me to bite down.

"I did not," I said, taking a step back. Of course, he followed.

His breath warmed my neck as he spoke. "You asked me once if I could read minds, and I told you I couldn't. That was true, but I can read bodies. I felt you pushing into me as we kissed. I sensed your heart beating faster, your blood pumping for me."

"You're wrong," I said, gulping as his energy increased.

He inched closer, his face almost touching mine. He inhaled slowly, making my entire body tingle as his breath tickled my neck below my ear.

"You're heart is beating faster now. I know when a woman is turned on. Do you think I've not done this before? Do you think your body isn't giving me clues? Your body temperature is rising, your heart pounding, your breathing is deeper. You can tell me you don't want me with your mouth, but your body tells me otherwise."

"My body is going to give you a swift kick between your legs if you continue," I growled, but by gods, he was right. My own body was betraying me, and I couldn't back up any farther. My calves were already touching the bed. Any farther backward, and I'd be flat on my back, a position I'd been in one too many times as far as Caspian was concerned and one I had a feeling he'd be happy for me to be in again.

"Whatever you say, princess, but in another week when I win that competition of yours, you'll be mine to kiss whenever I want...whenever you want."

He kissed my neck, sending my body into rhapsodies, before turning on his heel and stalking out, shutting the door behind him. It took a few seconds before I could get my body to move to bolt the door.

"Swit swoo," Nyre came out of the bathroom, a huge grin on her face. "Are you sure you don't want me to be a diversion for Milo while you and Caspian get it on?"

I threw a pillow at her as I tried to bring my breathing down to normal levels.

"I can't stand the guy," I said to her. "So he makes me hot, but he'd cut my throat in a heartbeat if there was something in it for him. Milo isn't like that. Milo would go to the ends of the earth for me."

"But Caspian makes you hot..."

Damn the dragon and her logic!

20TH JANUARY

Today was the day I was going to leave for Urbis. I'd wanted to do it yesterday, but Nyre had flown off before I'd even gotten a chance to speak to her about it. My plan was to go down to breakfast as normal and make sure everyone saw me. And that included Milo. I wanted to tell him where I was going, but I knew he'd want to come along. He would insist on it, and Nyre was too small to fly the two of us for long distances. If she was bigger and we could travel on her back, then maybe, but as it was, I was probably pushing it, asking her to take just me. I'd leave him a note and tell him how sorry I was. He'd understand...hopefully. With any luck, I'd find a way to stop my mother's curse, and best case scenario, my parents would be so overjoyed, they'd forget this whole wedding thing. They were only insisting on it because of some weird omen of dark times. I'd had enough people telling me that there had been some huge magical shift for me to believe it had happened, and I couldn't deny all the horrible stuff that had been going on in the past few weeks. But my mother's curse was part of that. If I could cure her, then maybe I could cure all of it. And I had a feeling that if I could find my birth mother and uncover the circumstances of my birth, then everything would unravel, and we could get back to how things used to be. I could date Milo and take my time getting to know him rather than being rushed into marriage. We could travel together and see the kingdoms rather than live with the threat of being torn apart, which is what was happening here. My only option was to go, and this was the day I was going to do it.

Milo wasn't stationed outside my room when I left, which was probably for the best. If I saw him, I'd probably break down and cry right in front of him, and he'd know something was going on. I didn't want to say goodbye to him. It felt too final. With luck, I could do what I set out to do within a couple of weeks tops. There would be no need for goodbyes, I'd be back before he knew it. I'd already written the letter telling him where I was going and who with. There would be no need to tell him why. He already knew why.

My father was at breakfast, which was unusual. In fact, the table was filled with people. All three of my brothers were there, as were Caspian and Charlotte. It seemed they were all waiting for me. For a second, I wondered if this was an intervention, but as I sat in my chair, they all began to tuck into their food.

I watched Caspian eating. Why did he have to be so damned gorgeous? Just being near him made my heart flutter, my fists clench, and my stomach turn. The thought of the kiss we shared yesterday flittered through my mind. It had been so good, phenomenal, in fact! He'd taken me to new heights and dropped me to new lows. How was it possible that one person could elicit so many reactions? He was fraying my nerves. He caught me looking and threw a wink my way, sending my stomach into another loop-the-loop. Color crept into my cheeks, so I turned to my father instead. I really did not need to be thinking of kissing Caspian.

"Why are you eating with us, Father?" I asked, more to steer my mind away from Caspian than anything else.

"Can't a father eat with his family?" he said, piling his plate with food. It was the first thing I'd seen him eat in weeks.

"Of course," I said, spooning some porridge into my own bowl. "It's just unusual, that's all."

"I know I've been absent of late," he said, adding some raspberries to his plate. "That's why I wanted to come to breakfast with you all. I've been so preoccupied that I've been putting my family last when I should have been putting you first. Isn't that right, Remy?"

He shuffled Remy's hair, who gave him a thumbs up while dripping his own porridge onto the table.

"Plus," he added, "if I hadn't come to breakfast, I wouldn't have met the lovely Charlotte here."

I refrained from reminding him that he'd already met Charlotte. He'd been too busy balling me out to notice. I wondered if anyone had told him why she was here. I didn't want him to know. The thought that my mother was somehow lost in some weird dream world was horrific, and he was dealing with enough. Hopefully he thought she was just visiting.

"You seem happy today," I mentioned hesitantly.

"I've got the best doctors in the kingdom arriving today, plus one from The Vale, one from Aboria, and I've even managed to snag a mage from Enchantia who is renowned for his work on curses. I'm positive your mother will be up and with us by dinnertime tonight."

I glanced across at Charlotte, who shook her head almost imperceptively. She didn't believe a mage or any amount of doctors could cure my mother. She didn't say anything, though, she just continued to eat.

"It wouldn't do to get your hopes up this early, Alec," Caspian said.

My father glared at him, and he recoiled. "I mean, I'm sure you're right, and these physicians will be able to help, but if they can't, it doesn't mean there isn't another way to save her."

He looked at me as he spoke.

"Exactly," I agreed.

"Nonsense," my father argued."Why would we need another way when I have the best? The best of the best."

So Charlotte and Caspian hadn't told my father her theory, which was just as well. It only strengthened my resolve to get to Urbis as soon as possible. If he was right, I wouldn't need to go, but I knew in my heart he wasn't. In a few hours, he would be heartbroken all over again. I couldn't bear it.

"We'll get her back Father," I said. "No matter what happens, we'll get her back."

After breakfast, I ran upstairs to pack. The sooner I left, the better. Once I was packed, I'd call Nyre down from the mountain and ask her to come. I pulled open drawers and took out clothes for the journey. It was cold here, so I needed lots of layers. I'd pulled out and refolded half my suitable clothes when there was a knock on the door.

"Hi, it's me, Charlotte."

After throwing all my nicely folded clothes in a heap at the bottom of my wardrobe, I opened the door.

"Hi, Charlotte. What can I do for you?"

She shuffled her feet nervously. "You told me the other day I needed the Dahlia treatment. I was wondering if you'd mind if she helped me today?"

I thought of all my clothes I'd have to refold and of all the doctors coming to see my father later. "I'm sorry, I don't have time right now. Maybe later?"

I felt bad, knowing there would be no later. She would find out I had left, and then she'd go home to Urbis... Urbis! She lived in Urbis. If anyone could help me there, it was her. I knew no one else there. If anyone would be able to help me in the weird walled city, it was her.

"Ok," I said, changing my mind. "Come with me. We need to find Dahlia."

A couple of hours playing dress up with Charlotte would give me the perfect excuse to learn about Urbis from her. I'd been to the city a few times, but always as a royal visitor. I needed to know the real city if I had any hope of finding my birth mother...or of finding Morpheus.

Dahlia had stationed herself in one of the castle admin offices. Well, it used to be an admin office. She'd had the desks and filing cabinets taken out and surrounded herself in wedding stuff. A small table overflowed with bridal magazines, and fabric samples covered the floor along with reams of ribbons, flowers, and goodness only knew what else.

"It looks like a wedding shop exploded in here," I commented, stepping over a pile of wedding favors.

"Half the kingdom is invited to the wedding," Dahlia said, pulling some magazines away from me as I stepped over to her. "Not to mention the royals from other kingdoms. It needs to be perfect. Draconis hasn't had a royal wedding for over eighteen years."

I rolled my eyes. "Why are so many people invited?"

She stared at me as though I'd just offered to cut her dog into pieces and serve it up instead of wedding cake.

"This is so pretty," Charlotte said, picking up one of the bridal magazines and holding up a picture of some model in a white dress.

"That was in my top ten, too," Dahlia beamed. "The seamstress has already started on the dress, but I guess we could ask her to change it a little. I like the long train. What do you think, Azia?"

I shrugged my shoulders. Who cared?

"Actually, I was wondering if you'd have time to help Charlotte here. She'd like a new outfit and her makeup redone.."

"I'm sorry," replied Dahlia, extending her arms out, indicating the mess around her. "I'm up to my eyeballs in wedding planning, and seeing as the bride refuses to help, I'm doing most of it myself."

She looked at me pointedly as I gave her my best ha-ha face.

"Charlotte is going to be my bridesmaid," I lied. "I'd like to do a trial run with her makeup."

"Oooh," Dahlia stood up quickly, sending a stack of invites toppling over. "In that case, come with me." She took Charlotte's hand and pulled her out of the room. I followed, expecting to end up in my room, but instead, she took her to my mother's dressing room.

The huge room was where my mother often got ready for parties and events. She wore no make-up most of the time owing to her natural beauty, but she enjoyed going all out when she got the chance.

Dahlia pulled out a chair in front of a mirror for Charlotte to sit in and pulled out her extensive makeup palette.

"It will make a refreshing change doing makeup on someone who actually wants it," she said, casting a meaningful glance my way. I rolled my eyes again.

"Can you get her a dress out?" Dahlia said, ignoring my eye-rolling. "Not one of yours. You have nothing bridesmaidy. Your mother has a collection of dresses she's never worn in that closet there." She was right. My mother was constantly being given expensive clothing as gifts, most of which she never wore. The things she liked, she kept in a closet in her room. Everything else went in here. She made it very clear to the castle staff that they could borrow any of the dresses they liked.

Pulling open the closet, I rifled through the dresses. They were all made with my mother in mind, but Charlotte was tall enough and slim enough to pull them off.

"What color?" I asked, figuring I'd try and get it right the first time rather than waste my day rifling through dresses.

"Red," both Dahlia and Charlotte said at the same time, then dissolved into giggles.

Charlotte was better at princessing than I was. I pulled a red dress from the closet and wondered what my mother would make of all this. She would love a daughter whom she could sit with and brush her hair whilst discussing new fashion trends.

"This one ok?" I asked, holding it up to the mirror.

"Beautiful," Charlotte said breathily.

I sat on a chair and waited as Charlotte was transformed from the mousy thing she was into a goddess. Dahlia really did know what she was doing. Charlotte sat patiently as Dahlia worked on her, but the excitement in her eyes as she was replaced by a woman of stunning beauty was clear to see.

I'd never had warm fuzzies from having my makeup done, but then again, to me, it was an obligation, a ritual I had to go through as the royal princess. To Charlotte who had nothing, this would be a treat. I almost envied her, her excitement in something I found dreary.

Once the makeup was done, Dalia began to work on Charlotte's hair. Pulling it from the ponytail it was in, Dahlia brushed it straight before beginning the process of braiding it into an elaborate up-do.

"How about leaving it down?" I asked, catching a glimpse

at my watch. I'd wanted to set off for Urbis early, but the day was quickly getting away from me.

"You need something special for your wedding," Dahlia said, pulling some diamond hair clips from her pocket.

Right, Charlotte was my bridesmaid.

An hour later, and Charlotte was ready to put the dress on. With Dahlia's and my help, she shimmied into the dress.

"Woah," I mouthed as I took in the vision of beauty in front of me. How had Caspian not noticed her before?

"You just need shoes and jewelry," Dahlia said. "Let me see what I can find."

"I have a necklace," I said. "You get the shoes, and I'll be back in a minute."

I raced out of the room and through the castle. The necklace my mother had left with the dwarves was still hidden in its box under my bed. I'd not brought it out since bringing it home the previous week.

The necklace was mine, a bit of my own history, but it was near useless to me sitting under my bed, and no matter how pretty it was, I couldn't think of a single reason I'd need to wear it in the near future. Royal parties were a little thin on the ground these days, with my wedding being the only thing penciled in on the royal calendar. I could hardly wear a ruby-red necklace with a white dress. Not that I planned to be around long enough to attend my wedding anyway.

When I got back to the dressing room, Charlotte and Dahlia were in the middle of the extremely important task of matching shoes with the dress. Her feet were a size smaller than my mother's, so Dahlia was reduced to scrunching up paper to fill the ends.

"We'll have to order something for the actual wedding," she said as she slipped a shoe on Charlotte's foot. For a second, it reminded me of the story of the queen of Arcadia,

Cinderella, who came to rule because of a shoe. I was willing to bet Cinderella didn't stuff her glass slipper with paper.

"Here," I said, passing the jewelry box to Charlotte.

She almost did a jig up and down on the spot in excitement. It was wonderful to watch. Her eyes opened wide with wonder as she opened the box. Inside the ruby necklace shone brightly, almost illuminating her face, but instead of the red they were before, now the rubies had changed into sparkling diamonds.

"Holy shit!" she breathed.

"Dragon fire!" I murmured at the change in the necklace.

"Beautiful," Dahlia mouthed.

We all spoke at the same time, but it was Charlotte's expression that interested me the most. The awe in her face had turned into something else, something bordering on shock.

"What is it?" I asked, pulling the box from her hands and gazing at the diamonds twinkling back at me. They had certainly not been diamonds before.

"How do you have the necklace of the gods?"

"What?" Dahlia looked at her with a perplexed expression, matching the turmoil inside me.

"I've seen this necklace before," Charlotte said, looking up at me, "but never on a human."

I snapped the box closed quickly. Suddenly it had become something I didn't want anyone to see. Something that elicited questions.

"Where did you get that from?" Dahlia asked, giving me a suspicious glare.

"I found it in the vault," I lied, hoping she wouldn't go down to check. "I guess it was given to my mother as a gift."

She nodded, seemingly satisfied with my answer, but I could see Charlotte wasn't.

"What do you mean, not human?" I whispered to her.

"These necklaces were given to people of high importance from the gods. Before now, I've only seen high fae wearing them. They hold powerful magic. I learned about them in my research."

I thanked her quickly, my mind whirring, and rushed the necklace back to my room.

Caspian had told me I wasn't a faerie like him. Of course, I wasn't. I didn't have the pointed ears of the fae, and yet, this was another hint that I wasn't human. If the gods gifted these necklaces to the fae, who else did they give them to? It was yet another mystery I needed to find out. I hid the necklace under the bed as someone knocked on my door. I opened it to find Charlotte.

"I'm sorry if I upset you back there. You ran off awfully quickly."

"You didn't," I lied. She didn't need to know that my mom had left this for me. I knew for sure, my mother wasn't a faerie, nor was she any other kind of magical creature. No the necklace might have been left for me by my adopted mom, but it had come from my birth mom. Maybe that's why my mother had hidden it away with the dwarves.

"Who else but fae owned these necklaces?" I asked her.

She shrugged, belying the interest in her eyes. "I don't know, but you can bet they would be powerfully magic. I think there's one in Enchantia."

Well, that made sense. Enchantia was the most magical of all the kingdoms.

"A mage owns one?"

"I believe so. My research didn't stretch to the mages of Enchantia. They aren't given out willy-nilly, not even to royals. I'm surprised that someone gave theirs to your mother, even if she is a queen."

A myriad of thoughts ran through my mind as I considered the necklace and how it had come to be in the dwarves' mine. Nothing made sense anymore, and something that should have sparked such joy only made me more nervous.

"Not half as surprised as I am," I said under my breath, linking my arm with hers. "Come on, let's go find Caspian. You're going to knock him out in that dress."

After scouring the castle, we finally found him in the dining room, waiting for dinner.

"Ah, there you are," he said as we walked in. "I've been meaning to come and find you. The Sentinel posted a picture of me, and I'm not sure you are going to like it."

Beside me, I felt Charlotte tense up. She looked absolutely stunning, and Caspian hadn't even looked her way.

"I don't care about what The Sentinel prints," I said, "Don't you think Charlotte is looking beautiful today?"

He grimaced, then cast his eyes at Charlotte.

"That's a nice dress," he commented, before swiveling his eyes back to me. "Now, what do you want to do about The Sentinel?"

Charlotte ran from the room, and I could hardly blame her.

"You are a total asshole, you know that, right? This is the second time in as many days you've done this," I snapped.

As I ran out of the room after Charlotte, I heard him shouting out behind me. "What did I do?"

I found Charlotte in her room, sobbing her heart out.

"The guy is an asshat, you know that, right?" I said, sitting beside her on the bed.

She smiled through a snot-streaked face. I stood up and found her a tissue, which she accepted gratefully.

"I just thought if I was beautiful, he'd want me."

"If you dated him, you'd have to fight for the mirror. The only person he thinks is beautiful is himself."

"He thinks you're beautiful."

"Purlease. He wants me because of who I am. He wouldn't

give me a second glance if I wasn't a princess. Besides, he's only marrying me as a favor to my father. I don't even think the guy likes me very much. He keeps trying to kill me."

"I doubt that," she said. "That's his way of showing love."

"His way of showing love is to kill his partner? What is he? A praying mantis?"

She laughed again. I left her to get out of her dress and take her make-up off and headed back to my room.

Looking down at my watch, I realized that the day had flown by, and my plans of heading to Urbis would have to be put off again. I didn't want to set off in the dark, and the evenings drew in awfully early in the winter. Closing the bedroom door behind me, I retrieved my messed up clothes from the wardrobe and began the laborious task of refolding them all. Less than a minute later, a knock at the door interrupted me.

Thinking it was Charlotte, I opened the door, but it wasn't Charlotte. Milo stood there, his face like thunder.

He threw today's newspaper down in front of me and walked away. When I looked down, I saw a picture of me on the cover. A picture of me and Caspian. We were kissing.

21ST JANUARY

Milo stood just outside my door, guarding it. It was his job, after all, but I knew he'd rather be anywhere but where he was. I'd hurt him badly, and no amount of talking to him had changed things. I'd brought him into my room, but there was no explaining away the photo of Caspian and I kissing. How the photographer had managed to capture the shot without either of us seeing, I'd never know, but he had, and now, the whole kingdom could see what a wretch I was.

I was lost to him now. It damn near broke my heart, but considering what I was about to do, it was probably for the best. Happily ever after for us was never in our future anyway. This heartbreak was always going to happen to both of us, it had just come sooner than expected.

Opening my window, I tried to drive thoughts of Milo from my mind. It was too painful to bear. Holding my hands out, I concentrated my magic. A small beam of light shot straight upward. My fear was that the guards in the courtyard would see me and come rushing up, but none of them even turned their heads my way, and I held the light.

I thought that maybe the dragons hadn't heard my call, but five minutes later, one of them landed on my window sill. The one I'd called for. Nyre ruffled her wings then hopped through the door. She'd transformed into her part-human self before the window was even shut.

"You ok?"

I nodded, running over to her, my forefinger extended over my lips.

"We have to whisper."

"Oh, wow. So exciting." her eyes widened. "What's happening? I love secrets."

It's not a secret exactly, I whispered, throwing a t-shirt at her to cover her bare chest. Her breasts were covered by her locks of long purple hair, but if anyone were to come in, they would wonder why she was in my room completely naked. The bottom half of her was almost more dragon than human with her iridescent purple scales, so it didn't really matter about covering her up there. Not that she seemed even the slightest bit bothered about her nakedness.

"You do realize that if I put this on, I'll only rip it to shreds when I transform back, right?"

I rolled my eyes and realized she was right. It must be awfully inconvenient being a shifter. Not that I'd seen any of them clothed when I was on the top of the mountain. Who needs clothes when you have beautiful scales and long hair to cover your wobbly bits, right?

She pulled the shirt over her head, not bothering to free her long hair from the neckline as I would have done. She looked remarkably cute in the thing. Much cuter than I ever had.

She picked up a book I'd left half-read on my bedside cabinet weeks before and flicked through the pages, absorbed in it as I often was with books. That particular book had sat there unloved and unlooked at for weeks, worry having taken over my nightly ritual of reading. I remembered it was a good book, but if anyone asked me now, I wouldn't be able to even begin to recall what it was about.

She appeared to be reading the words, but I wondered if she even knew how to read. Pulling the book away from her seemed cruel, but I had things to do. Things that couldn't wait. Carefully, I took the book from her hands.

"You can have this if you like."

Her eyes went wider still, elation plain on her face. She pulled the book back and hugged it to her chest.

"Thank you," she mouthed, her lips crinkling up at the side.

"I was wondering if you'd help me."

"In exchange for this beautiful paper thing?" she asked, holding the book up.

"No. The paper thing, the book. It's yours either way."

She nodded thoughtfully. "But you want help?"

"Yes. I need to get to Urbis. There are many ways to travel there, but I don't want anyone to stop me. Not even the king knows I want to venture there."

"You want me to take you on an adventure?"

I nodded. "I do. I could catch the train or Urbis Express, but both of those are public transport, and people would recognize me. I could take a horse, but it would take days to get there. I need to get there soon."

"Sounds good to me. Ooh. I've never been to a big city before. Do you know how to get there?"

Now that she'd mentioned it, I had no idea how to get to Urbis. I knew it was southwest of Draconis, but that was about it.

"Not exactly, but we could follow the train lines. The main line goes there. I know because I've traveled there in the royal carriage before."

"Can't you just travel in the royal carriage again?"

"Not without my father finding out."

She bounced on the bed, clapping her hands. "Well, goody for me! I get to come on the adventure. What is it we are going for?"

"I want to find my mother."

"I thought your mother was sick?" she asked, cocking her head to one side

"Not my mother, my birth mother. I think I was born in Urbis, and I need to go there and try and find out for sure."

"And you want to stay how long?"

I'd been thinking about my trip for a few days. Ever since I'd found out from Milo that I was born in Urbis, going there had occupied my every thought. Not only would going there give me a chance to find out about who I was and where I came from, it also meant I might just be able to solve another problem I had. I could hide out in Urbis while the competition was going on and miss my wedding. Yeah, my father was going to go ballistic. My leaving would do him no favors, but if I could find out what had happened to my mother, and figure out a way to save her, he would soon forgive me. He wouldn't care a jot about an abandoned wedding if my mother woke up. The competition was in a week's time and my wedding a few days after that. I figured it would take about four or five days to get to Urbis, but it was only a wild guess. I'd always slept on the train and never paid any attention to how long each journey took.

"Ten days. Four days there, Four back and maybe one or two in Urbis itself. I have a little money. Enough to stay in a hotel or something."

"You call this a little money?" she asked, taking in the grandeur of the room. It embarrassed me the way everyone thought I was rich because of the stuff I had. Okay, yes, I had a lot of fine things that cost a lot of money, but it was all useless if I didn't have the freedom to go with it. I had to stash money away to get the small amount needed to spend ten days in Urbis. I had to smash a childhood piggy bank, which I'd had since before I could remember, and even then, it was barely enough for a couple of days in a hotel. I couldn't sell any of my things, nor could I use them to buy other things like food. So I'd spent the last few days searching the castle for cash. For a place as filled to the brim with riches as it was, it was surprisingly difficult to find any actual cash. Going back down to the vault was not an option. I'd already made Hestor suspicious once this week, and I could hardly do it again. So I had to be more creative, searching down the backs of sofas and into the pockets of my parents' coats hanging in the closet. Okay, yes, it was stealing, but I found such small amounts in each place I looked, my father wouldn't notice anything missing. It took a full three days to gather the amount I had, and I wasn't sure it would be enough, but I was counting on Nyre being able to forage for a lot of her own food, and while we were out in the countryside, maybe some food for me too.

"I don't know much about Urbis," Nyre said. "But I think it will take a lot longer than four days. I will have to rest. I'm not a train or an airship. I'm a dragon. I will need to take frequent rests, and I will need to sleep. Am I right in thinking you slept on the train when you went before? Because I can't carry you while you sleep. When you sleep, I'll be sleeping too."

She was right, of course. I'd assumed she would be this relentless machine, but she was a living creature.

"I guess we will take longer then...maybe two weeks?"

"And you'll not want to fly over any towns or cities. People will see us, and word will get back."

I slumped down on my bed. In my active imagination, this had all been so easy. Find money, call Nyre, and just go.

Now, she was filling my head with problems I didn't even know I'd have, and what was worse, she was right about every single one of them.

I'd only packed a small bag, thinking I'd not be gone too long, but it looked like I'd have to rethink the whole thing.

"Would you mind waiting until I repacked. It won't take a minute."

"I can wait for you, but you will need to wait for me too. I cannot just leave the colony. My father would come looking for me."

Vasuki! I'd forgotten about him too. My mind was just such a mess of things that my plan was a total disaster.

"Maybe I shouldn't do this..." I said, feeling dejected. Maybe I should accept my fate and marry whoever won the competition. It would keep my father happy if nothing else.

"Don't be silly. We can do this. I'll come back tonight."

I nodded. There was something about Nyre that made me feel better about the whole thing. She quickly turned back into a dragon, ripping the t-shirt to shreds as she had predicted and flew out of the window.

The door bursting open behind me had me turning my head.

"Who were you talking to?"

Caspian strolled into the room as though he owned the place. Something he was particularly skilled at.

"How dare you come into my room." I cast my eyes down to the bed, knowing I'd hidden my sword underneath it.

He followed my line of sight.

"Don't worry. You will not need your sword. I only came in because I thought you were in trouble. Who was it, by the way? Do you have someone hiding in the bathroom? It didn't sound like a man, but one can never be too sure."

"I wasn't talking to anyone," I snapped back as he

wandered over to the bathroom door and peered into the bathroom.

"Hmmm. What a mess you keep your room in," he said, picking up a piece of the remnants of t-shirt that Nyre left behind. "When we are married, I'll expect you to keep your home much better than this."

I strode over to him, pushing against his chest. "If you don't like my house, feel free to leave...Any time."

I slammed the door in his face, anger surging through me.

I spent the afternoon outside in the woods where I'd been practicing with Milo. He wasn't outside my door when I left, and I didn't ask Jack where he was. I didn't want to know. If Jack told me he'd gone home, I knew I'd run to his house and drag the pain out longer than necessary for both of us.

Without Milo, fighting seemed pointless, with only the snow to keep me company, but anger spurred me on, forcing me to carry on the practice. I was almost as good as Milo now. I'd proved that. I was a match for him. I fought invisible foes all afternoon until hunger forced me to leave the beauty of our fighting place and move indoors.

After a quick change of clothes in my bedroom, I headed down to dinner. I had plenty of time before Nyre was to come pick me up, so I decided to eat my fill. I didn't know when I'd be eating again.

For the first time in what felt forever, my whole family was at the dinner table. The only person missing was my mother. Her empty seat was all the more obvious now that the others were filled.

"Where have you been all day?" My father asked as I sat down in my place. Immediately, a servant brought over a plate of meat and vegetables.

"I was outside getting some fresh air, Father."

"In this weather?" he indicated the window where the

snow fell freely. I would need to take some warm clothing with me if I were to survive.

"I like the snow," I answered, digging into the food. My belly was happy with the warmth.

"At least, we won't have to worry about the dragons in this weather," Hollis said. "They'd be mad to attack with the snow the way it is."

I paused and looked up at Hollis, who continued eating. "Attack?"

My father waved his hand dismissively. "Not to worry, Azia. The dragons are quiet once again. We've not had an attack in over a week. The wall is still being erected to keep folk out. Maybe that's all they wanted."

"But we still need to be vigilant, Father," Hollis added." Just because they haven't attacked for a while, doesn't mean they won't attack."

"They won't!" I said, a little too urgently. Both my younger brothers' eyes swiveled my way.

"And how do you know?"

I was saved having to answer by my father chipping in.

"She doesn't. I don't want to hear any more about the dragons. I've done all I can with them. I've got enough on my plate at the moment without all this nonsense. Your mother isn't getting any better. The doctors I've had brought in have been looking at her all day, prodding and poking her, and none of them can find a damned thing wrong with her. All of my troops are back, and not a single spindle has been found. And now, I've got this bloody competition to worry about. The reporters are hounding me every second of the day, and quite frankly, I'm sick of it all!"

He stood up, throwing his napkin down on the table and stormed out, his face as black as thunder.

"It really would have been easier if you'd just married Caspian, "Hollis said.

"Are you blaming me for all this?"

"You did start this ridiculous competition," Ash added. "It's taking up so much of Father's time that he can't concentrate on the important stuff."

"And my life isn't important?" I shot back. "Would either of you married someone you hated out of duty?"

Both of my brothers nodded their heads. "I would do anything for my kingdom," Hollis said proudly.

Standing up, I glared at him. "Well, look who's suddenly all patriotic. Three weeks ago, you couldn't have cared less, but now that Father has made the pair of you soldiers, you think you are better than the rest of us." I slammed my fist on the table, upsetting my uneaten meal. I was starving, but anger trumped that. I followed suit with my father and left the dining room, slamming the door as I went.

Anger raged within me, and I wanted nothing more than to go back to my room, shutting everyone out, but having not eaten all day, I had the perfect excuse to head to the kitchens. I would need food for the journey. While Nyre would be able to kill small animals and eat them raw, that wasn't an option for me, and I wasn't confident enough of my fire-making skills.

The kitchen was winding down, with the chefs leaving and the clean-up staff getting to work on their parts. Nobody paid me any mind as I ran into the larder and filled a cloth bag with food. Nyre was tiny, so I couldn't take much, nor could I take anything heavy. Having Vasuki or Emba to carry me on their backs would have been the better option, but I knew better than to ask them.

Back in my room, I emptied the bag of food onto the bed and sorted it into my backpack. Putting in the clothes I would need, I also pulled out my boots and a thick coat that would keep me warm on the nights I'd have to sleep outside. Then, all I had to do was wait. Nyre knew better than to come to me while it was still light, so I whiled away the hours staring out of the window, waiting for the sun to fall in the sky. At least, the snow was abating. It was beautiful to watch the large flakes falling, but the cold would be a killer if I wasn't prepared. My hope was that we'd find shelter on the nights we were venturing to and from Urbis. Sheds and barns would keep the snow from us, and we'd be able to snuggle down in the hay. At least, that was my plan. This would all have been easier in the summer months where we could have slept under the stars or even in a normal Draconian winter, which were usually very mild. The snow, however beautiful, reminded me that this was not normal weather and was brought about by the darkness caused by the witch. My hope was that if I found out where I came from, I could find out what had happened to my mother and wake her up. My father had not found her spindle, and I know he would have knocked on every single door in Draconis to search. Which meant that Derillen was no longer in the kingdom.

Before Nyre came, I went to see my mother. My father sat next to her. He barely looked up as I entered the room.

"I'm sorry about my outburst, Azia," he said, his voice cracking. "I thought that if I brought the best doctors here, they'd find out what was wrong with her. Not even the mage from Enchantia knew."

I walked over to him and cradled his head as he sobbed.

"I'll make this better, Father."

He nodded in my arms, but I could tell he didn't believe me. Why would he? If the best doctors in the land couldn't cure mother, why would he think I could.

"I think maybe you should go and talk to Caspian and Charlotte," I said. I couldn't tell him where I was going, he'd only stop me, but once he found out I'd gone, I wanted him to know the truth. I'd written him a letter to explain, which was back in my room, but talking to Charlotte about Morpheus would make it more real to him like it had to me. Charlotte really believed that Morpheus was involved, and I had no reason not to believe her. Hopefully, my father would too. "They think they might know how to get her back."

"How?" He asked, his eyes bloodshot from crying.

"Go see them," I urged. I pulled back from him and bent over to kiss my mother's cheek. I'd bring her back or die trying.

I left the room and headed back to mine, only to find Nyre waiting for me on the bed. She hadn't shifted out of her dragon form, so I picked up my backpack, threw my coat on, and climbed up onto the little window sill.

Nyre's talons caught in the back of my coat, and with a tug, we were both flying. It took a moment to get used to the sensation and to get over my crippling fear of being dropped. Once again, I wondered if it would have been better to go to the dragons and ask for help from a bigger one. One I could sit on the back of, but I liked Nyre, and I trusted her. I would just have to trust her with not dropping me because this was going to be a long journey. We flew over the courtyard, and she circled around the side of the castle to head in a south-easterly direction. We were almost over the outer wall of the castle when something zipped past my ear. At first, I thought the snow had started again, but this came too quickly for snow, and it came from below us, not above. Nyre rocked to the side as another thing flew past. This time I saw what it was. It was an arrow. My father's men were shooting at us. Jacob stood at the front of them and sent another arrow our way.

"Go faster!" I screamed at Nyre, but it was too late. She was already plummeting to the ground, and I was falling along with her. This was it. We were both going to die. As the ground rushed up towards me with dizzying speed, I knew then that I wouldn't be able save my mother on this trip. I'd had one chance, and now thanks to Jacob, I never would. My mother would die, and as I slammed to the ground and everything went black, I knew I would beat her in death.

Continue the adventure in Goddess of Flames

A NOTE FROM THE AUTHOR

The Kingdom of Fairytales authors hope you enjoyed this new way of reading. We don't think that a series has ever been set with one chapter a day thought a whole year before and we hope we did it justice.

With this in mind, please leave a review, but when you do, remember that these books were always meant to be short breaks in your day and the blurb reflects that.

We would LOVE it if you can drop us a few words on Amazon

Review here

AFTER THE HAPPILY EVER AFTER…

There is more to these stories. You want to know what happens next right? Fast forward eighteen years…

Pick up book one now

PREQUEL

SLEEPING BEAUTY

1. Queen of Dragons
2. Heiress of Embers
3. Throne of Fury
4. Goddess of Flames

LITTLE MERMAID

5. Queen of Mermaids
6. Heiress of the Sea
7. Throne of Change
8. Goddess of Water

RED RIDING HOOD

9. King of Wolves

10. Heir of the Curse
11. Throne of Night
12. God of Shifters

RAPUNZEL

13. King of Devotion
14. Heir of Thorns
15. Throne of Enchantment
16. God of Loyalty

RUMPELSTILTSKIN

17. Queen of Unicorns
18. Heiress of Gold
19. Throne of Sacrifice
20. Goddess of Loss

BEAUTY AND THE BEAST

21. King of Beasts
22. Heir of Beauty
23. Throne of Betrayal
24. God of Illusion

ALADDIN

25. Queen of the Sun
26. Heiress of Shadows
27. Throne of the Phoenix
28. Goddess of Fire

CINDERELLA

29. Queen of Song
30. Heiress of Melody
31. Throne of Symphony
32. Goddess of Harmony

ALICE IN WONDERLAND

33. Queen of Clockwork
34. Heiress of Delusion
35. Throne of Cards
36. Goddess of Hearts

WIZARD OF OZ

37. King of Traitors
38. Heir of Fugitives
39. Throne of Emeralds
40. God of Storms

SNOW WHITE

41. Queen of Reflections
42. Heiress of Mirrors
43. Throne of Wands
44. Goddess of Magic

PETER PAN

45. Queen of Skies
46. Heiress of Stars
47. Throne of Feathers
48. Goddess of Air

URBIS

49. Kingdom of Royalty
50. Kingdom of Power
51. Kingdom of Fairytales
52. Kingdom of Ever After

JOIN US

Would you like FREE Kingdom of Fairytales Coloring pages? Click the link below to pick your free gift up.

Kingdom of Fairytales FREE gift

Check the Kingdom of Fairytales website for competitions, news and info on all the books and authors

Kingdom of Fairytales Website

Or Join us on our Kingdom of Fairytales Facebook page for fun, games and author takeovers

Still want more? Completely immerse yourself in the Kingdom of Fairytales experience and pick up exclusive offers and gifts

Become a Patron

THE KINGDOM OF FAIRYTALES TEAM

These books would not be written without a great many people. Here is our team:

Many thanks to those who have made this possible.

Thank you to Rhi Parkes without whom, this series would never have come about.

Thanks to all the authors.

J.A. Armitage, Audrey Rich, B. Kristen Mcmichael, Emma Savant, Jennifer Ellision, Scarlett Kol, R. Castro, Margo Ryerkerk, Zara Quentin, Laura Greenwood and Anne Stryker

Also thank you to our amazing Beta team

Nadine Peterse-Vrijhof, Diane Major, Kalli Bunch and Stephanie Pittser.

Thanks to our Proof Reader

Tina Merritt

Thank you to our Patrons

Gigi Nickerson, Amanda Hurst & Coralee Butterfield

ABOUT THE AUTHOR

J.A lives in a total fantasy world (because reality is boring right?) When she's not writing all the crazy fun in her head, she can be found eating cake, designing pretty pictures and hanging upside down from the tallest climbing frame in the local playground while her children look on in embarrassment. She's travelled the world working as everything from a banana picker in Australia to a Pantomime clown, has climbed to the top of Mount Kilimanjaro and the bottom of the Grand Canyon and once gave birth to a surrogate baby for a friend of hers.

She spends way too much time gossiping on facebook and if you want to be part of her Reading Army, where you'll get lots of freebies, exclusive sneak peeks and super secret sales, join up here

https://www.subscribepage.com/v7o8k4

Somehow she finds time to write.

Printed in Great Britain
by Amazon

60696956R00071